LOVE TOUCH

"Mia, where do you go when you need love?"

Adam touched her curls and wanted to lose his fingers in the thickness of her hair.

"I don't go anywhere. I don't need love," she whispered.

Her clear polished fingernails were the only thing he dared to touch as they fluttered against her earlobe.

Adam drew them to his lips, letting his kiss linger. When he drew them away, he helped her stand. His arms slid around her with a naturalness that was comfortable.

"Everybody needs love. It's not something you can buy, but something the right person has to bring out in you." He tilted her chin slightly back until her raised eyes met his. "You're worthy of love. I only hope that I can get to be the one who shows you what's inside you."

"You don't know me," Mia said.

"You're right. I don't." His eyes grew serious, touched with flames of desire. "I want us to get to know one another better. One of these days, you're going to have to take a chance."

NOW OR NEVER

Carmen Green

P

Pinnacle Books
Kensington Publishing Corp.

http://www.pinnaclebooks.com

PINNACLE BOOKS are published by

Kensington Publishing Corp.
850 Third Avenue
New York, NY 10022

Pinnacle, the P logo, and Arabesque are Reg. U.S. Pat. & TM
Off.

First Printing: November, 1996

Printed in the United States of America

10 9 8 7 6 5 4 3 2 1

Acknowledgments

I would like to thank these extra special people.
Monty, Jeremy, Danielle, and Christina, I appreciate all
your love, support and faith.
To my mother, Mildred, father, Bryant, brothers Bryant
and Kenneth, and sisters Stacy, Whitney, and Yvonne,
for believing in me.
To Martrice and Mona, for being excellent
cheerleaders.
And to Jenni, Wendy, and Karen, the best critique group
around.

Chapter 1

"Mr. Webster, it's four o'clock. Will you be going out *there* today?"

Adam Webster ceased the rhythmic tapping on the computer keys and glanced at his gold wristwatch, checking the time. Standing, he raised his long arms in the air and shrugged his shoulders to ease the soreness.

"Just a minute, Angela," he responded, and heard the soft click of the disconnecting line. He rotated his arms, then massaged his tired eyes before walking to the corner window to contemplate his decision.

Bleak, he thought as he looked out.

The skies were filled with swollen gray clouds, waiting to unleash another bout of rain on the already-soaked citizens of Atlanta, Georgia. Pausing, he counted the number of consecutive days it had rained this July. Today would make the twelfth day. However, no matter how terrible the weather, he felt compelled to visit the quiet place.

Thoughtful, he gazed out until the discreet intercom beeped again, interrupting his reverie. Moving back to the desk, he pressed the button.

"Angela, I will be going to the cemetery for a short visit. Were there any messages?"

"Yes, sir. Shall I bring them in?"

"Yes. Come in."

Angela marched into the office and planted herself firmly in front of his desk. Settling himself once again in the leather chair, Adam slung one leg across his thigh, tented his fingers, and waited for her to begin.

"Angela?" he called after a long moment of silence, eyeing her quizzically. "What are the messages?"

"Yes sir. There were two. One is from J.R., and he specifically asked me to read it to you." She began to recite, imitating J.R.'s voice. "Why have you been dissin' me? If you want to stay homies, come to the club Saturday night at seven o'clock. Otherwise, you're to the curb. Signed, Me."

Deep laughter shook him as he listened to the message from his best friend, Jonathan Rio Johnson, known to everyone as J.R.

Adam took a moment to think back over his twenty-one year friendship with J.R. From the moment he stepped out of the moving van with his mother and found J.R. sitting on his porch, they had been best friends. His mother filled a void for J.R., whose own mother had walked away one day and never returned.

For Adam it wasn't that easy. While J.R.'s father was a good man, Pops could never take his father's place and he didn't try. Adam loved and respected him for being a positive role model during his impressionable years, although he still felt alone and isolated sometimes.

Angela waved another pink message slip to recapture his attention. Nodding his head, he indicated for her to continue. She huffed and lifted her chin indignantly.

"What would you like me to do with this one? It's from Candice Walker . . . yes sir, the circular file." Angela seemed to glean a certain pleasure when she dropped the pink, lined paper into the trash can.

"Sir, she's left four messages in as many days, and she's been incredibly nasty. Shall I continue to tell her you're unavailable?"

"No. I'm going to put a stop to this once and for all. If she calls again, go ahead and put her through."

Angela nodded and shifted from foot to foot.

"Was there anything else?" Usually he couldn't stop her from rushing back to her desk to finalize the daily reports. Today she obviously had something on her mind.

"As a matter of fact, there is. Mr. Webster, Adam," she said, her voice softening as she tugged on the sleeve of her cardigan sweater. "I'm worried about you. It's been months since Grace died. Why do you have to go today? You were there last Thursday and the Thursday before. Sir, don't you think it's time to start seeing your friends, or begin to travel again? It's not too late to pick up where you left off, before all this happened."

Angela clasped her hands together, her voice taking on a helpful tone. "Maybe even start dating somebody steady . . . that way, you won't be so . . . lonely." She smiled when his surprised expression turned to exasperation. "Don't make that face, sir. I may be old, but I know when my boss is dating, and when he's not. We've been together too long for me not to know."

Adam's patience was thinning on the subject, although his expression revealed none of his inner turmoil or the hollow emptiness that plagued him since he had finally come to terms with his mother's death.

"Anyway, the forecast for today's weather is terrible. It's going to rain again, all day—"

"Angela," he broke in, unable to stand another moment of the suffocating concern, "I agree I haven't seen my friends, and I will soon. Yes, I have been visiting the cemetery too much, and yes, I will begin to travel again."

Adam stood, glancing at Angela before walking into the

mahogany-paneled closet, returning with his smoke-gray suit coat. He shrugged into it as he gave instructions.

"Make copies of my travel itinerary. It's on my calendar. And send it to the wholesalers on the yearly forecast. I'll begin next week. Also, I would appreciate it if you could make some sense out of my desk."

Angela walked past him to the closet with a sad smile on her creased face. Adam understood her concern for him, but he didn't want to be coddled. He would date when he found the right woman.

"Hey, Ange?"

Angela's gray-streaked head popped out of the closet, a look of curiosity on her face.

"Don't worry about me. I like being single. But if the right girl comes along, well then . . ." His voice softened and he smoothed down the lapels of his jacket.

"Then I'll consider myself a very lucky man."

She handed him the umbrella. "Take this. That expensive suit can't hold too much water."

He sighed when she started tugging on her sweater, fastening the buttons then taking them apart. She wasn't through giving advice, and he prepared himself.

"I only worry about you because I've seen you grow up and mature, and since you bought out Aberdeens you've done very well for yourself. You're a fine, responsible young man who needs a family. That's what Grace would have wanted."

"Angela," he said, his voice taking on an authoritative edge. "Let me worry about the details of my private life." He waited, then added, "Okay?"

"Yes, sir."

Adam looked at her bent head and regretted speaking so harshly to her. But this preoccupation with his private life had to stop.

"Mr. Webster?"

"Angela," he countered.

"Don't forget your wallet."

He winked at her, took the long leather billfold, and inserted it in his breast pocket.

"Thank you," he said softly. "Have a good evening, Angela."

"Goodnight, Mr. Webster."

Opening the golf size umbrella which flaunted a green embossed W, for Webster's Wholesalers, Adam strode with a purposeful lift in his step to his black Jeep Grand Cherokee and got in. Since his destination was only a short distance from work, he allowed his thoughts to drift while he drove across the paved, narrow streets.

Four months. He sighed.

It had been four months since his mother died. Adam grew pensive when he remembered how Hodgkin's disease had robbed her of her body and eventually her life.

Her apology to him was still fresh in his mind. He'd gone to visit her at Crawford Long Hospital, bringing her favorite roses. Though heavily sedated, she was lucid and greeted him warmly.

Grace looked almost serene with her head bound in a bright scarf, and she had even gotten her nails polished. Her vanity was still intact, and that pleased him. There was part of his mother that the cancer could not touch. The respirator had been removed and she could talk on her own.

He leaned close to hear her soft voice.

"Indulge me, Adam. I know how you hate for me to meddle in your affairs, but I want to talk to you.

Son, I'm sorry I won't live long enough to see my grandchildren or meet your wife. You've devoted these last six months to taking care of me, and I love you for it. But I worry that you've spent too much time with me. That's why things didn't work out with you and Candice."

"Mom, my problems with Candice have nothing to do with you."

"Your father used to say that he had half a heart until he met me. Once we got together, he was whole.

"The other half of your heart awaits. You'll find her soon."

Three days later she died, wearing the favorite flannel pajamas she'd had J.R. bring to her at the hospital.

Adam pushed the turn-signal down and waited for the light to change. This would be his last visit for awhile. As much as he hated to admit it, Angela was right. It was time for him to get on with his life.

Crushed gravel kicked up under the wheels upon his arrival at the cemetery parking lot. He circled the lot, choosing from its vast emptiness a parking space near his destination.

Temporarily, the rain had stopped, yet he picked up the umbrella, anyway, and began the short walk to his mother's resting place.

Kneeling beside the grave, he brushed away the windblown leaves and twigs. He had grown accustomed to the solitude of the cemetery, and spoke softly.

"Hi, Mom. I've been fine. Work is going well. Soon I'll be traveling, so I don't know when I'll get back out here again. I've been coming out here for the past few weeks because of a pact I made with J.R. years ago. We said that we would always take care of you and Pops, no matter what." He chuckled softly, picking up a brown leaf. He twirled it in his hand, then began speaking again.

"I'm going to take your advice, Mom. I bet you never thought you would hear me say those words. I'm picking up the pieces of my life and going on. Although I would do it all again. You gave me the best years of your life." He swallowed and continued. "I love you, Mom."

Adam lowered his voice and stood respectfully when a tall woman walked past his mother's tombstone, oblivious of him. Her ebony hair was swept up in a loose twist from which several long tendrils escaped. She sniffled quietly and turned down another grassy path, away from him.

Adam watched until she disappeared, then knelt back down.

Something about her made him snap his head up and follow her with his eyes to see where she was going.

He could hear the distant rolling thunder, and knew his time was even more limited. Heavy mist had begun to descend, and from the west he could see dark clouds moving ominously toward him.

He brushed his hand over the gray tombstone and whispered the words that lay on his heart. "Mom, I don't know if I ever thanked you for sending me to school to study horticulture, or for pushing me to be the very best I could be. You provided me with a great life and I'm grateful. I hope you and Dad are together. Give him a high five for me."

Peacefulness enveloped him as he brushed the grave free of more windblown leaves. Absently, he inserted them in his pocket and walked toward the cemetery exit, the damp Bermuda grass making his shoes slick. Adam had shortened his stride to maintain his balance when he saw the woman who'd passed him earlier, about ten yards off to his right.

Even from that distance he could see how beautiful she was. She had dark, chocolate-colored skin that was smooth and unblemished. He couldn't tell how long her hair was because it was loosely bound, but he guessed it ended somewhere down the middle of her back because of the long curls that escaped by her ears and temple.

Two glittering diamonds pierced each ear. She lifted her hand and touched her cheek, and he watched the slow movement, mesmerized. There was something about her that kept him rooted, transfixed.

She knelt at a small headstone and stared at it. She didn't cry or move. Occasionally she would look into the sky, and he thought perhaps she was praying, but her eyes remained open, her hands by her side.

Thunder growled a great rumbling sound. Then it boomed, seeming to shake the earth around them. The black clouds that were once in the distance had closed in, turning the mist to a light drizzle.

Thin raindrops slid off his suit, but he wasn't aware of them. His attention was still captivated by her. He walked closer, and her quivering chin let him know when she began to cry. Silent tears blended into the rain, and his chest constricted.

Adam looked down at his shoes, which had begun to collect water, and realized he still held the umbrella in his hand.

Pressing the button, he walked over to the lonely woman and held it above her. She was sobbing now, her shoulders shaking, her eyes closed as her hands clutched the little cement headstone.

To witness her suffering was nearly unbearable, and he wanted to leave, but couldn't. Her personal pain was so deep that it touched a cavern of protection within him. He just wanted to take her in his arms and comfort her.

Rain pounded the nylon umbrella, making a rhythmic drumming sound, yet she still hadn't moved.

Adam watched the driving rain mold her white silk blouse to her body. Beneath was black lace, and he cast his eyes down. The short black suede skirt disagreed with the rain and blanched, ruined from the moisture.

His eyes were drawn back to her face when she covered her mouth with her hand and tried to stifle her sobs. Drawn to know who she grieved for, he adjusted the umbrella slightly and glanced at the small cement square. His earlier peacefulness was replaced with sorrow.

It was the headstone for a child.

Nikki Jacobs. Although the date indicated two years had passed since the child's death, Adam noted that today was the child's birthday. She was probably the child's mother. He stood for an indeterminate amount of time, patiently shielding her with the umbrella, saddened for her.

Lightning crisscrossed the sky and Adam looked up, growing concerned. He stepped closer to the woman, and for the first time since he'd been there she seemed to be aware of his presence.

She glanced over her shoulder, her puffy eyes laced with fear. She leaned away from him, then pushed herself up.

Adam took in the condition of her rain-soaked clothes again as she slowly backed away. He slid his damp jacket off and offered it to her.

"Your clothes are all wet. Take this," he said, extending his arm. The umbrella still covered him, but she had stepped from within its confines and was being pounded. Under the weight of the water, her hair tumbled down and hung dripping over her shoulders and back.

Suspiciously she eyed him, then tentatively reached for the jacket. He was relieved when she slipped it on and covered herself. Adam kept his voice low. "You can step back under the umbrella. I won't bite."

"No," she croaked, her voice harsh with emotion. "I'm fine. Please leave me alone."

"I apologize for the intrusion. I was leaving when I saw you, and then you began to cry. I thought I could . . ."

Adam let the words drift off. He didn't know what to say. All the common phrases seemed trite and overused.

Unashamed of her grief, she didn't bother to stop the flow of tears as she stepped closer to him.

"What were you going to say? That you wished you could bring her back, or God has a special place in heaven for children? Well I don't want to hear that. I want her back. Can you do that? Can anybody do that for me?" she lashed out.

"No Ma'am, I can't. But if I could I would." Her bottom lip quivered and she squeezed her eyes shut. Lightning sizzled the sky. Her voice was sullen.

"Please leave us alone. I want to be alone with my baby." She turned her back, dismissing him.

Adam couldn't move. His body refused to obey her request, and his feet stayed rooted to the ground as if held there by a terrific magnetic force.

"I understand," he said softly. "As I said before, I don't

want to intrude. I just thought I could do something to help. Even if it's only being here.''

Unable to reach out for fear of frightening her, Adam simply watched as she moved further away from him.

The rain intensified. It didn't matter that he held the umbrella. He was getting soaked, too. Water stains had begun to grow up his legs toward his knees, contrasting the wet and dry areas of his suit.

''This rain doesn't seem as if it's going to let up. Maybe you could come back another day,'' he said, and hoped she would take his suggestion.

It wasn't the rain that was driving him away, but her desire to be alone.

''You can keep the umbrella.''

Adam cautiously reached out and touched her hand just as a bolt of lightning ignited the dark sky. Brilliant light flashed, illuminating her pain-racked face, and his heart shattered into a million pieces.

Her fingers curled around his, and her naked grief touched his soul.

''She didn't deserve to die.''

Their eyes connected, and Adam opened his arms. For a moment he was unsure if she would accept his support, but her hesitation lasted only a millisecond.

Before he could believe what happened she was against him, her arms wrapped around his waist, her head tucked into his shoulder. Crying.

Adam released the umbrella to the ground, and enveloped the woman in a strong, protective embrace. He didn't care that the downpour from the sky was relentless, and water dropped off his nose and landed on her shoulder.

Her tears melted his heart. He comforted her, rocking her gently, speaking in soothing tones, caressing her back. ''It's okay to cry.''

They swayed together, his strong arms bracing her firmly against his chest as his knees bent slightly to make a perfect fit of their bodies. There weren't many women who were as tall as he. While she didn't meet the eye level of his six-foot, three inch frame, she couldn't have been more than six inches shorter.

Distantly, he thought about how he liked tall women.

Very much.

Eventually, the rain began to peter out. And the pounding noise was gone, leaving only her sniffles and intermittent hiccups.

As his body absorbed her final tremors, he became more and more aware of how athletic her body felt. The full length of her was pressed against him, and he prayed his personal admiration for her figure would not reveal itself in a physical way.

Unexplainable feelings of protectiveness engulfed him as he stood in the desolate cemetery wanting to kiss her tears away, wanting to make promises that would soothe her soul. He felt the beat of her heart, strong and consistent, as he gently rubbed her back. He wanted to keep her there forever.

So many questions rushed through his mind. Why was she here alone? Where was her family? How could anyone leave her alone on a day like today—her dead child's birthday?

Her breathing pattern changed as the final hiccups subsided, yet her head rested comfortably in the space made for her in his chest.

Reluctant to release her, Adam held her slightly away from him. The profound effect she had on him shocked him. He knew their meeting in this time and place was for a reason. He felt something sparking to life inside him. Something he didn't want to let go of. He had to know her. Yet how?

A small catch in his throat stopped his breathing momentarily as the warm color of her eyes captivated him.

"Did you drive here?"

Shaking her head, she indicated no.

"May I offer you a ride, then?"

Again, she shook her head.

"Then how will you get home? It's not safe for a woman alone near sundown."

Eyeing him with ill-disguised suspicion, she moved from within his embrace and bent low to retrieve her purse. She backed away a few feet, then turned and strode quickly down the grass to the path leading to the entrance of the cemetery.

Adam watched her walk away. His mind shouted for him to do something. Somewhere deep inside himself, he knew he had to see her again.

Easily matching her stride, he caught up to her as she stopped at the corner just outside the cemetery gate.

"Do you have a name? I'm Adam Webster."

To her silence, he tried again. "Are you sure I can't drop you somewhere?"

He knew the look she gave him was meant to stop his blood from circulating. Adam realized his insistence must sound threatening, and he tried to clarify himself.

"I don't mean to scare you. Look, I just let you cry into my best suit. I even offered you my umbrella. I don't mean you any harm."

She never breathed a word as she silently perused a sodden schedule taken from a pocket of her ruined skirt.

The rumbling hiss of the bus made him realize she would board it and ride out of his life forever.

The double-paned bus doors slapped open, and he looked at the driver in silent appeal. Adam's hand blocked the doors' closing as he watched her insert the correct fare. The quick movement of the door handle by the driver indicated they were ready to leave.

The doors slid, and for the first time since they left the cemetery she acknowledged him by looking at him. Adam felt a quickening in his middle when he heard her throaty voice.

"Mia Jacobs."

The doors slapped shut and Adam stared at the lumbering vehicle until it became a small dot of blended lights, wondering if he would ever see Mia Jacobs again.

Chapter 2

Is being alone an impossibility? Mia wondered as she quickly brushed past passengers who, like her, had disembarked the bus at the train station. She glanced around, noting most were holding Braves banners or flags.

The family next to her grumbled about the game being rained out. *Just my luck.* She sighed, and shivered from her cold, damp clothes. She yearned for a hot bath and the comfort of being home, alone.

Boarding the train, she found an unoccupied aisle seat and draped her long wet hair over her right shoulder, hiding her face from the man who sat across the aisle. He stared openly at her disheveled appearance, and she wondered if he thought she was homeless.

Mia sighed. What did it matter what he thought? It had been a long night. The man turned and faced forward, and her thoughts flew to her painful breakdown.

Nostalgic memories of Nikki's birth flooded her and Mia remembered how it felt to hold her for the first time.

Mia bit her lip, holding back the tears. All her plans for their life evaporated with her death. And the sad reality was that she would never have children again.

What hurt worse than knowing she could never hold the child again was the shroud of suspicion that hung over Derrick, her ex-husband, concerning her death.

The train swayed around the track and pulled into the station, and a throng of passengers entered.

Mia sat stoically, holding her breath as several people approached, looking for seats. She lowered her eyes and didn't breathe until they moved on to other available chairs. Relieved, she let her thoughts return to the days after Nikki's death.

Derrick had been questioned all night by the police, but had been released early that next day. He had walked into their custom-built home in the early morning hours, not to give comfort, but to deliver one final blow.

"I want a divorce," he said, his voice empty of emotion. It hadn't begun to slur from alcohol, she noticed through her grief induced haze. That was unlike his usual intoxicated state.

"I told you I never wanted children," he went on. "So I can't even say I'm sorry. You brought this on yourself." He tipped up the tumbler of Scotch, and walked into their bedroom, but Mia couldn't bring herself to follow.

It hurt too much. She sat at the dining room table and didn't look up until he threw his keys on the table. He held the garment bag in one hand and suitcase in the other.

"My attorney will be in contact with you."

He returned to Chicago two days before the funeral. The divorce was swift. Derrick demanded and won spousal support for one year. Even her lawyer shafted her. She couldn't prove Derrick had any influence over him, but he took advantage of her grief and advised her to sign over to Derrick their home in Chicago and brand new Mercedes.

Mia had to sell their Atlanta home to pay off debts, then cash in all her bonds and the savings plan from work to pay off the others. It was just as well. She couldn't live in the house without Nikki.

Her life in shambles, she took an indefinite leave of absence from Scottish Rite Medical Center and tried to recover from the tragedies that surrounded her.

Bracing herself against the cool night wind, Mia left the train and hurried the short distance to her car, parked in the lot. Jumping in, she started the old Cutlass Supreme and headed home.

As she gathered the lapels of the coat around her, the scent of earthy cologne drifted up her nostrils, dragging images of the tall, dark-skinned man through her mind.

He was so tall. Mia's body warmed against the wetness of the clothes as thoughts of his long arms locked around her and his words soothed her, making her grieving easier to bear.

The place between his shoulder and neck felt especially right. She had wanted to stay there for a long time.

Preoccupied, Mia drove until a light changed from green to red in a split second. The car skidded on the slick pavement, coming to a stop just under the light, next to one of Atlanta's Finest.

Snapping her head forward, she prayed he wouldn't pull her over. She couldn't afford a ticket. Relief poured over her when he pulled away, and she turned into her apartment complex.

Mia backed into her designated parking space, and exited the car. Slowly she trudged up the stairs to her door. Securing the dead bolt behind her in the studio apartment, she flipped on the light and dragged her arm from the jacket, the lining plastered to her skin.

She threw the soggy coat into the laundry basket and then tossed in the silk blouse and suede skirt. Mia shivered as she hurried to cover her goose-pimpled nakedness and put on a kettle of water for some hot cocoa.

Running a tub of water, she dragged the portable radio to the door of the bathroom, tuning it to a mellow station.

The people upstairs were quiet for once, and she was thankful. She just wasn't in the mood for Mariachi music tonight.

The kettle hissed, and she stirred the water over the brown powder, then took it to the tub with her.

She slid into the heated water, welcoming its soothing warmth, and reclined against the porcelain. Intermittently, she sipped her cocoa, letting it warm her insides. The radio played softly in the background and she closed her eyes, willing her body to relax.

Behind her lids, the man slid into focus. He had a muscular chest and lean waist, obvious when the full length of his body had pressed against hers. His face scratched her lightly when his chin slid across her cheek, and she remembered his words when he pressed his lips to her ear. *"It's going to be all right. I'm here."*

It wouldn't be a problem adjusting to that kind of support, Mia thought as she scrubbed her body vigorously.

She rinsed herself, then drained the tub and wrapped her body in a bright orange beach towel. She wound another around her head and sat on the corner of the bed, the lotion bottle turned upside down over her hand.

Miserably, she shook her head, ending the fantasy. Letting a strange man fondle you in a cemetery does not a relationship make.

"Oh God," she exclaimed when another dose of reality hit her. She had been fondling him, too.

Mia exhaled sharply as lotion poured over her hand, landing in droplets on the sectional Oriental rug.

Fingering up the droplets, she massaged them into the rug, then dressed in long pajama pants and top. Her eyes wandered over the apartment as she picked up the radio and returned it to the kitchen counter that served as a breakfast bar as well.

She had tried to section off the studio to make a one bedroom apartment, but had little success because of the huge, four-poster canopied bed that commanded too much space.

She knew it was too big, that a twin or full size bed would have been sufficient for her needs, but she couldn't resist buying it. It was the only luxury she allowed herself when the divorce had come through.

Mia retrieved her cocoa cup from the bathtub and walked

to the kitchen. She rinsed it, then walked out to straighten the small living room area that held a couch, love seat, shelf and, end table.

She pushed the rollaway cart which held the television into the cramped space by the door and straightened the cover on the armchair.

Mia's eyes slid to the laundry basket which stood outside the bathroom door, and a fluttering in her stomach let nervous butterflies loose.

Tentatively, she took steps toward the wrinkled suit coat whose lined sleeve was turned inside out, hanging out of the basket. "Don't let it be true," she mumbled as she pushed aside the wet skirt and blouse, and pulled it out. She held it upside down, staring at it in disbelief.

"Ouch!" Mia searched the floor for the object that had landed on her foot. The towel, which had been wrapped around her head turban style, began to unravel, and she fought with it, trying to see the brown leather billfold.

Gripping it, she eased it open and stared at the driver's license photo of the man from the cemetery. He was smiling at her. His voice seemed to sneak into the room and swirl around her.

I'm Adam Webster.

"Go away," she groaned, closing her eyes. "I don't need this."

Mia paced, trying to shake the awakening feelings inside her. American Express Gold Card, Visa, and various other credit cards filled the slots, and she fingered through them, looking for a business card.

She flipped through the pockets and found two hundred dollars, but no phone number. Carefully, she reinserted everything and straightened the jacket on a hanger, placing the wallet in the side pocket.

There's nothing more to do, she thought, pushing her strange reaction to his driver's license photo aside. *I'm just tired,* she thought on her way out of the bathroom, where she put the hanger.

The shrill ring of the phone stopped her, and she hurried to the table by the bed, then hesitated before answering. *It might be him.*

"Hello?" Mia hated the way her voice pitched higher.

"Hey, Mia, it's me. I was concerned about you, since you left the health club early today."

Her boss's voice filled her ears and she sighed, relieved, then grew frustrated.

"What is it, today? Do I have a sign around my neck that says 'helpless female in need of a man to save me'? I'm fine, Jon. Is there anything else?"

"You know what, Mia? I don't need your attitude. I was just concerned. I thought you might be sick or something. Seeing that you're in high spirits, I'll leave you alone."

"Jon, wait!" she called into the phone, regretting her outburst. The whole thing with the man in the cemetery and now finding his wallet was wreaking havoc with her good sense.

"I'm sorry. It's just been a bad day." She paused. "Jon?"

He let out a long, slow breath. "We all have bad days, Mia. It's forgotten," he said, making her feel slightly better.

"Are you still at the health club?"

His voice was muffled with his hand over the phone. Then he answered, "No. We're at my father's house. Star is here with me and she wants to talk to you. Hold on."

The phone transferred and Mia sat cross-legged on her bed, waiting.

"Mia?"

"Hi, Star. I didn't mean to yell at Jon," she said apologetically.

"He bruises, but he doesn't break," she said in a forgiving tone. "Mia, why didn't you wait for me? I'm your best friend. I would have gone with you to the cemetery." Star's voice eased. "Are you okay? Want some company?"

"I don't know, and yes," Mia answered, trying to cover her broken sob with a laugh.

"I'm on my way. Have you eaten?"

"No, and stop trying to feed me. I'm really not that hungry."

"Good, I'll pick up some Chinese," she said, ignoring Mia's response.

The towel fell to her shoulders and she left it there.

"Will Jon mind?"

"No," Star assured. "We've been over here since he got off. Besides, he and his father are involved in a serious Dominoes game with some neighbors."

Just then Mia heard the explosion of laughter and voices as the men disagreed over a move. Good-natured ribbing filtered through the receiver, bringing up painful memories of her own family and the loneliness she used to feel, wishing she hadn't been an only child. The sneaking cloak of depression enveloped her.

"Mia," Jon's voice clamored into the receiver. It was so loud it made her jump.

"I'm still here," she said, holding the phone away a short distance.

"Pops is having his annual fish fry two weeks from Friday. Rain or shine. Say you'll come, okay? He's been bugging me. Says he wants to meet my new aerobics instructor."

Mia chuckled at the round of *oooh's* that echoed in the background.

"If she's pretty . . ." somebody said.

"She won't want you," the other responded, which made the whole group break up. Even Jon laughed.

"I would love to come."

"Pops," Jon yelled over the din of noise. "She said she'll come."

More teasing rang in her ears, and the dark depression passed. "I'm glad you're laughing again, Mia. I'll check you out tomorrow. Peace, out."

"Peace, Jon."

Sliding the phone on the base, Mia snapped into action. She blew dry her hair and plugged in the hot curlers. Dragging the laundry basket into the bathroom, she dropped the silk shirt into the sink as she read the tag. Washable. May be dry cleaned. Medium.

I used to be a sixteen, she thought feeling a small amount of pride at her decreased size. Pulling the skirt from the basket, she read its label: dry clean only. 10.

She held it up. It had been ruined by the rain. Regretfully, she dropped it into the garbage can.

Maybe that's why Derrick left, she thought to herself as she kneaded the blouse in the soapy water. No. He drank himself into his problems. It wasn't my weight.

After she rinsed the blouse she hung it over the tub.

Star knocked on the door, calling her name.

"Come in," she said to her friend, who came in laden with brown square bags.

Star laid them on the counter and threw her Coach bag on the couch. She gave Mia a big, sisterly hug.

"How are you?"

That's all it took. Her eyes watered and she walked to the counter, fidgeting with the bags.

The usual tormenting pain didn't come this time. Just a dull, dry ache. "It's getting better," she said, and opened the bag, avoiding Star's penetrating gaze.

"Did you get caught in the rain?"

"Yeah. I was hoping you would volunteer to curl my hair for me."

When she looked up she could read the sympathy in Star's green eyes, and was ashamed. She didn't want anyone to feel sorry for her. Going to the cemetery tonight was good, she told herself. It would help her move to the next phase of her life. Whatever that might be.

"Girl, you're gonna have to pay me some serious cash to straighten out that mess," Star teased, lightening the mood.

"Come on, let's eat first. Then we'll get to the hair."

"All you do is eat, and don't gain an ounce," Mia grumbled, putting half the portion on her plate that Star had on hers.

Star laughed and settled on the sofa, one foot beneath her.

"I'm thirty-five, and I'm high on life. My metabolism is faster because of it."

"High on life?" Mia questioned, disbelieving. "That's an interesting concept." She dug into her food and chewed slowly.

Star ate fast, chewing little, talking a lot.

"Remember when we first met? You were upstairs in the club, struggling to lose your last twenty or so pounds. What did I tell you?"

"Hey lady, get your fat butt off that treadmill, you're hogging it?" Mia's tone was dry, and Star laughed, pointing her fork at her.

"Besides that." She answered for Mia. "That you needed a change. Your body can grow accustomed to too much of the same thing. And what happened when you stopped walking for one month and took the step aerobics class?" She answered again for her. "You lost it."

Star shoved a forkful of food into her mouth and swallowed. "You have to do things in moderation. Exercise, work, eating. Everything," she emphasized, "but sex. Do that all the time."

Mia laughed at Star's quirky expression. "So?"

"So what's my point?" Star asked. "That you've been in a rut. You're trapped by things in your past. If you start to let go of them one at a time, before you know it different things will happen for you."

At thirty-five, Star could easily pass for a woman ten years younger.

They were complete opposites, but she had been a good friend from the first day they met. Mia was thankful to her and Jon for helping her when she desperately needed friends and a job.

Jon helped her pass the tests to become a certified aerobics instructor, and now she was the choreographer for the entire staff of instructors at his health club. It was a change from pediatric medicine, but one she welcomed. She didn't know how she would have made it had it not been for them.

"Did you think about him, while you were out there today?"

For a moment Mia stiffened and looked at her friend. She then realized Star was not speaking of the man from the cemetery, but Derrick.

"A little," she confessed.

"Don't waste your time, Mia. He was a louse. Anybody that could walk out on a grieving woman and blame her for his problems is not good enough for her."

Mia pushed her food around on her plate. "I always thought when a couple had problems, they worked them out. But I've realized that it's rare when people stick it out for the long haul."

"It makes you think we should burn those fairy tale books about the handsome prince, huh?"

"Oh, I don't know." She sighed and set her plate beside her. "You seemed to have found your prince."

"I have," she agreed. "You will, too."

Mia rolled her eyes, taking her plate to the kitchen. When she spoke, her voice was filled with conviction. "I won't ever get myself into something like that again. Relationships aren't for me."

Star followed, rinsing them both off. Mia brought the curlers out of the bathroom and plugged them in at the outlet by the closet. She dragged the armchair over.

Star sectioned her hair into small parts and began wrapping it around the hot curlers.

"One bad relationship isn't the end of the world. You should have more faith in yourself. You deserve to be happy. Be still," Star muttered, blowing on the curlers. She worked them loose and took another section of hair.

"I thought I used good judgment the first time. But I blame myself for a lot of the problems. It's not easy being a two profession family. Plus, Derrick was never keen on kids. He would never commit to a specific time. He always said later, and the one time we didn't use protection I got pregnant. He never forgave me for that."

"Girl, he never forgave you for getting the job here in

Atlanta, or for his getting fired from his job. I didn't know him, but from what you've said he doesn't sound very nice, or like he deserved you.''

Mia sighed. It was the truth. She couldn't remember many nice things about him, either.

Star curled her hair in silence and soon it was secured at the back of her head in its normal ponytail. "I can't believe all my hard work is in that hair bow," she said, disgusted.

"Thanks, hon," Mia said, and hugged her, following her out the door and waiting until she was securely in her car.

The electric window of the Acura rolled down and Star stuck her head out.

"You gotta get out of your comfort zone and try some of life. It's not bad out here.''

"Goodnight, Star," Mia said patiently, a smile curving her lips.

The sky was clear and the constellations shone brilliantly. Star tooted the horn and she turned. "Try it. You might like it.''

With a quick wave, she was gone.

Mia cleaned the dishes and brushed her teeth. She adjusted the lace curtain that hung around her canopy bed and crawled under the covers.

She punched the pillows into position and settled in, reflecting on her life. One whole life, lived in thirty short years. Now I can go on. But to what, she wondered as her eyes lowered sleepily. Saving lives and helping children had once been purposeful and fulfilling.

Then marriage and having Nikki made it all complete.

But now it was all gone. To love and lose it all again would be too much. Mia turned onto her side and drifted to sleep with images of Nikki comforting her.

Late into the night visions of Adam Webster dominated her dreams, making her toss and kick at the covers until dawn's early light.

Getting out of bed an hour early, Mia made up her mind.

The only way to stop thinking about him is to find him and return his things. Then I'll never have to see him again.

Walking into the club Saturday evening, Adam hoisted his gym bag more firmly onto his shoulder. Ever since the encounter with Mia in the cemetery, he had thought of little else. The last two days had been merciless.

Although trying to concentrate during the inventory meeting, Adam found his mind drifting, thinking of her.

Her long, rain-slicked ebony hair and whiskey-colored eyes made him yearn to see her again. Several times during the meeting he groaned aloud, until Angela gave him a glass of water and some aspirin for his discomfort.

Unfortunately, what ailed him couldn't be cured by two little pills.

Seeing her again. That's what he needed more than anything else.

His search up to this point had been unsuccessful. There were eighty-four M. Jacobs in the phone directory, and it was taking some time to contact them all.

So far, there were three possibilities that kept him hopeful and confused. The first being that he just hadn't found her yet. Second, she wasn't listed. Third, she gave him the wrong name.

The third scared him the most. But something about her made him feel that she hadn't deceived him. Nor would she intentionally walk off with his suit coat.

Other troubling thoughts plagued him. As he'd passed the stone on his way back to his car, he'd read the inscription imprinted on its base. "With love, Mom and Dad." He couldn't recall if she wore a wedding ring. Why hadn't he been at the cemetery with his wife? His stomach clenched. He didn't want her to be married. He just wanted to see her again.

Locking his bag in the men's locker room, Adam walked into the club office and teased in a smooth voice, "Hey beautiful, when are you going to marry me?"

"When you going to seriously ask me?" quipped Esther Henderson, the eldest member of the club, and the in-house secretary.

"Where you been? I ain't seen you around for a while."

Sheepishly, he ducked his head. She was a straight shooter, but had a kind heart.

"I've been around," he said. "I just had to take care of some business lately. But I'm all right."

Adam tried to divert the attention away from himself. "How's Mr. Henderson?"

"Don't go changing up on me. How come you ain't came by for some fried fish? Too good for fried foods?"

He could tell her feelings were hurt, so he hopped the small gate and planted a kiss on her heavily rouged cheek.

"Esther," he said, placating. "I'll come by soon."

She yelled at him as he walked out the door. "J.R.'s in the aerobic studio. But there's a class going on now. Don't you stick your head in there. She don't like late-comers who don't warm up properly."

Adam waved his acknowledgment and walked back through the lobby of the health club.

New indoor-outdoor carpeting lined the floors and two glass enclosed racquetball courts had been added off to the right.

He headed down the long hall past leather lounging couches and tropical fish tanks, stopping at the gym. The new floors shone bright and even the baskets had been restrung.

There were lots of unfamiliar faces, he noted as he headed for the studio. J.R. must be doing very well for himself.

Adam cracked the door open and heard her voice first. "Travel, repeater three's." His heart thrummed a crazy beat as he listened more closely.

"Travel, over the top. Kick, corner to corner," she instructed. He couldn't believe it.

Her voice was a rich sandalwood. In fact, he knew he'd only heard it one place before.

Time and again she issued commands, her breath catching in between, staying in time with the music.

Heat flashed through him like a bright bulb before he inched the door wider. He inhaled deeply, then exhaled slowly. There was only one way to find out.

Adam yanked on the door with more force than necessary and stepped inside.

He didn't see Mia Jacobs.

The stage from where the instructor usually led the class was empty.

Feeling foolish, he started to back out. Then he spotted her. She stepped on a platform with another person, doing a track and field movement.

Her face glistened with sweat as she bounced in time to the funky beat and issued step commands.

"Walk around," she said, and the class responded.

Totally absorbed in her work, she concentrated on the precise movement as she took the class through its cardiovascular paces. Adam studied her lithe body as she praised the class when they moved in perfect formation.

Her long dark hair that he had seen soaking wet was covered with a billed cap, and a microphone headset swung in front of her mouth.

Her voice rang out, thrilling him.

"Everybody doin' okay?"

"Whew," they responded enthusiastically.

His eyes followed the curves of the blue and white striped workout outfit which clung to her lean figure.

The back navy strip disappeared between her rounded bottom, and it was hard for him to draw his eyes away.

They slid lower, over her thighs which were encased in short white bike shorts. Her long dark legs ended in high leather aerobic sneakers.

The cotton lining of his nylon jogging suit stuck to him as he grew warm watching her.

Involuntarily, Adam licked his lips and was disappointed

that the red cherry lipstick on her mouth was not there. He eased along the wall until he was at the back of the studio.

"Bas . . . ic," she called as she caught his movement.

The "basic step" command stuck in her throat, and the class bobbed up and down from the missed call. Adam leaned against the wall and crossed his feet at the ankles, inserting his hands in his pants pocket. He felt sure she recognized him, but he detected something else in her eyes that wasn't easily identifiable.

The class eventually got back on track, but he never noticed because his attention was focused completely on Mia.

After a ten minute cool down the class ended, and she was stopped by several members. Adam took that opportunity to move closer. Spotting J.R., he walked toward him, but was headed off when she broke away from the crowd.

"Are you following me?" she demanded.

"No," he said, taking in her defensive posture.

"Then how did you know I was here?" Her voice quivered and she seemed to be fighting for control.

"I didn't," he said, facing her. Adam couldn't remember the last fight he had, but he smelled one brewing and he wanted to head it off. "I've been trying to find you because—"

"I knew it," she exploded. "You're some kind of pervert, aren't you?" She didn't wait for an answer before she hurried to Jon.

"Jon, I want you to call the police on this man. He's a weirdo." Her voice raised, and her eyes darted over him. "I saw him at the cemetery, and now he's found me at my job."

J.R. looked at him questioningly as Mia dragged him between them. "Why are you still standing there? Call the police!"

"What are you talking about?" J.R. turned to Mia with an incredulous look.

Adam cooled under her suspicious scrutiny and said nothing.

"I already told you," she said, reaching a soprano pitch. "Thursday he followed me at the cemetery, and now he shows up here today. That's no coincidence."

Turning to Adam, she pointed at him menacingly, anger lacing her voice. "I'm not afraid of you. I don't know why you're here, but if you touch me you're going to be very sorry you met me. Forget it," she said, and threw up her hands. "I'll call myself."

She picked up her bag and stormed toward the door. Adam finally spoke up.

"Are you calling them now? Because I hope you can explain why you stole my suit coat and wallet."

"I didn't steal it," she sputtered incredulously. "Y-You gave me that coat. How was I to know you were irresponsible enough to give your wallet to a stranger?"

"Time out," J.R. demanded, and grabbed them both by the arm. Neither budged. Mia placed both her hands firmly on her hips and Adam imitated her motion, glaring back at her.

"Take this off the floor and to the office now," J.R. growled.

They both moved with obvious reluctance to his office.

"Both of you SIT!" he commanded once they were behind the closed door.

Adam casually leaned against the wall as Mia warily stared at him, taking the chair. J.R. tipped his head toward him, and Adam finally sat down, listening to J.R.'s voice thundering in the small room. "Would somebody like to tell me what in the hell is going on here?"

They both exploded at once.

"He's a pervert,"

"She's crazy,"

"Hold it!" J.R.'s exasperation was evident. He expelled his breath and dragged his hands slowly over his face. Smoothing his hair, J.R. obviously worked to gain patience. "You're both trippin'. If you don't calmly tell me what's going on," he held up his hands, "one at a time, I'm going to leave and you guys can kill each other." Turning to Adam, J.R. gave one last try.

"Adam, what's up?"

"She's a thief. Call the cops."

J.R. rolled his eyes and slapped his hands on the desk.

Mia jumped up so quickly that the chair went crashing to the floor. Her husky voice rang through the tiny office. "You're a liar! You followed *me,* not the other way around. What kind of pervert are you to go feeling up grieving women in cemeteries? You gave me that coat and I had every intention of giving it back, but now I don't think I will. I'll just throw it all in the trash, where its owner belongs!"

As he stared at her, Adam's jaw jumped. He raised out of his chair. His voice dropped to a caressing pitch. "Was I really feeling you up? If I *were, feeling you,*" he emphasized, "you would know. I comforted you. You needed someone and I was there."

He moved within inches of her. The pulse at her temple was clearly defined.

"You weren't thinking I was so perverted when you had your arms around me, were you?"

"Whoa, hold up. Will you please back up?" J.R. spoke to Adam.

Adam moved away, his control restored.

"Jon, what's going on here? How do you know him?" Mia's voice was weak. She looked at her boss.

"Mia, this is Adam Webster, my best friend. He lived next door to me practically all my life and he's cool people."

J.R. turned to him. "Adam, this is Mia Jacobs, my new step aerobics instructor. She's been here for about six months, and if you had brought your butt in here before, you would have met her."

Adam accepted the scold with a shrug.

Her suspicious glare lessened, but didn't completely disappear.

"Adam is a good guy. He lost someone, too. That's why he was in the cemetery. He's definitely not someone who preys on women in unusual places."

Mia moved to the fallen chair and righted it, then picked up her bag. She had thrown it in the corner, long ago.

Adam watched her walk to the door. "I need my things tonight."

Her hand stopped midair.

"Can I pick them up?"

"No," she answered without hesitation, keeping her back to him. "I'll bring them tomorrow and give them to Jon." She turned the knob and opened the door.

"Miss Jacobs, I need them tonight," he said, matter-of-factly.

He couldn't just let her walk out like she had the other night. There was so much he wanted to know. Like why she was so vulnerable and scared. Why had she been grieving alone? And why she was so angry now.

They both turned when J.R. spoke. "Mia, how about if Star and Adam and I stop by together? That way he can get his things tonight, and I promise he won't be a pervert, at least not while we're there."

Adam shot him a withering look for attempting humor at that moment. Then he swung his eyes back to Mia, who stared him up and down for a long, long time.

"All right."

She walked out the door without a backward glance at either of them. Adam felt his shoulders sag from relief.

"What in the—What just happened here?" J.R. demanded.

"I don't know," Adam said. "I'll be ready at nine o'clock. Tell Star don't be late."

Chapter 3

Adam worked out with an intensity he hadn't experienced in a while. Twenty-four repetitions per side was all his body could stand as he pumped the sixty-pound weights, pushing himself physically to the limit, trying to alleviate the stress.

Her anger frustrated him. Mainly because he didn't know enough about her to draw an easy conclusion. He had to find out more.

J.R. peeked his head into the weight room and held his hands up in mock surrender. "Is it safe to come in?"

Laughing at the goofy look on J.R.'s light-skinned face, Adam gestured for him to enter. He laid the weight by his foot and adjusted the black gloves on his hands.

"I didn't do anything to her. I saw her crying on the ground in the rain at the cemetery, and I gave her my suit coat. That's all."

"You like her, don't you?"

Adam and J.R. stared at each other and Adam shrugged his shoulders. "I can't explain it, man. I met this woman at a *cemetery*. Isn't that kind of—, morbid?"

J.R. laughed. "It would be, if it weren't Mia."

Adam checked his watch and stood abruptly. "I'm too old for a chaperone, but she's calling the shots. Where's Star?"

"Talking to Esther," J.R. said. "Anytime Esther gets with Star, they never shut up." Adam grunted his agreement and replaced the weights on the stand.

He grabbed his bag and headed for the door with J.R. behind him. Their progress to the front doors of the club was slow, as J.R. stopped several times to talk with members and staff of the club. Because he was so personable and easy to talk to, the club was a huge success.

Adam clapped J.R. on the back. "The club looks good, J.R. I know I haven't been around in a while. But don't give up on me."

After they shared a quiet moment, J.R. said, "I know you've been busy, but I miss Grace, too."

Touched by J.R.'s uncustomary show of emotion, he reached out and squeezed his shoulder. "I understand."

"You going back out to the cemetery anytime, soon?"

"No," Adam said. "I've got to move on. I'll be going out of town soon, and getting into a few other things, if I can work it out." His grin told J.R. it wasn't business, but a lady, on his mind.

"You can work it out," J.R. said confidently. "But I hope you have a lot of patience. Mia is rare."

Adam pushed open the door, then stopped.

"Tell me one thing." He zipped his jacket and lifted his bag to his shoulder. "Is she married?"

"J.R. Johnson, please come to the office, J.R. Johnson."

J.R. smiled and jogged away. "See you at a quarter till."

Adam gestured to stop him, then changed his mind. He would find out soon enough.

Standing between the White Lightnin' rosebush and Bonica bushes in the lighted garden, Adam heard J.R. and Star push open the sliding glass door from the house and enter the garden.

Using special shears, he finished snipping the blooms and hurried toward them. Every tree, shrub and bush in the one acre garden had been planted there by his hands, and he was very proud of it.

"Come on, Romeo," J.R. yelled, teasing. "You're going to be late for Cinderella."

Adam followed the stone path back to the house, careful not to brush his pants against any of the damp leaves. He kissed Star and presented her with a beautiful cutting. "This is for you," he said, taking her hand gallantly and draping it over his arm.

"Thanks, sweetie. Ignore him." She stuck her tongue out at J.R. "He never could get his fairy tales straight. You have the right idea. Flowers are the way to a girl's heart."

They walked back through the house, where Adam set the alarm, then went out the front door to Star's car.

"Star, tell me about her," he said from the back seat.

"What do you want to know?" she said, turning to face him.

"Is she married? Where is she from? What happened to her little girl?"

"Well," Star said evasively, "I can only answer one. She's from Chicago. I'll let her tell you what she wants you to know. She's a very private person."

"You're doing me wrong," he accused lightly. "I thought we were friends."

"We are. But she's been hurt bad in the past and she's very protective about who she confides in. I can tell you this much. She used to work at Scottish Rite," she offered to his obvious curiosity.

"The children's medical center?"

"That's the one."

"What did she do for them?"

Silent communication passed between J.R. and Star, and she turned around in her seat.

"I'll let her tell you that. I'll just say this much. Consider

yourself privileged that she's even going to let you in her
apartment.''

Adam drew back at this. ''What does that mean?''

''She's sworn off men.''

''For how long?'' he asked, listening intently.

''Forever.''

The slamming car door caused Mia's stomach to jump nervously with anticipation. *There's nothing to be nervous about,*
she reminded herself.

Pausing after hearing the knock, she forced herself to walk
over slowly and turn the handle. She opened the door slightly
and peered into Adam's mocha-colored eyes. *Somehow they
weren't this attractive before,* she thought as she stared at him.

''Hi. May I come in?''

''Oh, yes. Sorry.''

Embarrassed, Mia opened the door wider and stepped back.
The tiny apartment seemed to shrink as he entered.

He stood just inside the entrance, and for the first time she
had an opportunity to really look at him.

He had the smoothest, darkest skin that she'd ever seen on
a man. His hair peaked slightly in the front and was wavy to
the nape of his neck. But his eyes were what attracted her most.
They were warm and inviting.

He openly accepted her perusal with an easy smile of pearly
white teeth.

Everything seemed brighter, sharper, and smelled better as
the intoxicating scent of his cologne swirled around her.

''Hello, Mia.'' Jon waved to capture her attention. ''We're
here, too.''

Jon and Star stepped around Adam's tall, muscular frame
and she cleared her throat anxiously.

''Hi. I didn't see you.''

Adam moved by her side, letting the others in so they could
close the door.

Mia rocked on the heels and balls of her feet and jabbed her hands in her jeans pocket.

Everyone stared from one to the other.

"Can we sit down?" Adam asked when the room fell silent.

"S—sure," Mia said, feeling foolish that she hadn't thought of it. Mia rushed to sit in the armchair, but Jon and Star beat her to it. They tumbled on top of each other, with Star barely making Jon's lap and not the floor.

There wasn't any place else to sit but by Adam on the small couch. Mia felt as if someone had shut off all the air in the room. She walked over, and six eyes watched her sit.

His broad shoulders touched hers, and his long legs stretched out against her thigh. "Sorry, there isn't much room," he said, rewarding her with a beautiful grin.

"What's so funny?" she asked crossly of Jon and Star.

"Nothing," they chimed together, smiling foolishly.

Mia was relieved when Jon took charge after another lengthy silence. "Mia, remember Adam? He has a nasty habit of lurking in cemeteries, wanting to soothe grieving women. He also likes to play in dirt and travel to places unknown to humans, to find rare things nobody but him cares about." The tension in the air lessened under J.R.'s humor.

"Adam, this is Mia, who is new at the health club, and she's the best aerobics instructor in the whole state of Georgia. Okay, introductions over. Now give it to her."

Adam creased his brow, looking as puzzled as she felt. She peered closer when Jon started flapping his vest.

"You know," he said, through clenched teeth and a shake of his head.

"Right, right."

Butterflies danced in her stomach when Adam pulled three roses from inside. "These are for you. I'd like to be friends." He lifted her hand from her lap and placed the roses in her palm.

His rough hands against her soft one sent thrilling needles of pleasure through her. They were calloused from hard work, yet still gentle. She remembered how gentle they could be, and felt her heart quickening its beat.

"Thank you," she managed to whisper. Mia gently touched the petals and sniffed the strong fragrance of the bloom. It was intoxicating. Or was it his cologne that had her wanting to swoon?

"You're welcome. I hope you like them," he said.

"I don't know if I have anything to put them in. I hope they don't die," she said shyly, and walked to the kitchen. Jon and Star whispered to each other, ignoring them.

"You don't have to worry about hurting them." She watched as he stroked the leaves lovingly. "These roses are sturdy, from the oldest rosebushes in the world. They can sustain any kind of weather, and despite their delicate beauty they have hearty roots and a fine fragrance. They're beautiful, just like you."

Her knees turned to Jell-O, and she reached for the counter to steady herself. The roses lay halfway between them. She reached for the cabinet door above her head.

"You seem to know a lot about flowers," she said, trying to act normal. "Do you work with them?" Mia was surprised when he started laughing.

"Did I say something funny?" The tips of her ears burned as he watched her open cabinets, looking for a vase. *Just don't turn around.* Something warned. She did, and her gaze flew right back to his.

She pulled down an Atlanta Hawks glass and filled it half full. It was impossible to stick them in the water with him watching!

The glass clattered, water spilling everywhere.

"I'm making a mess," she said, grabbing the towel to cover her embarrassment. She caught the stream of water that was heading for the floor in one long swipe.

"Here, let me," he said, and filled her kitchen when he stepped in. *This place is made for children,* she silently fumed, *not two full size adults.*

Jon coughed raucously from across the room, breaking the

spell. Mia smoothed her hair down, a nervous gesture she had been unable to break since she was a small child. She didn't know how many more appreciative looks and easy smiles she could take from Mister Helpful.

"Is anybody hungry?" J.R. asked, and didn't wait for a response. "Come on, Star." He grabbed Star's hand and headed for the door. "Let's give them a chance to talk and go get something to eat. Guys, we'll be right back with some chow and some cards."

"Wait," Mia protested, but they were out the door before she could stop them. Her friends had deserted her. Especially Star.

Mia looked out the corner of her eye at Adam, who now relaxed comfortably on her couch, looking around the apartment. She took a deep breath and ran her hands down her sweatshirt and folded her arms across her chest.

The armchair was free, and she settled in it.

"You have a nice place," he said, not mentioning the unoccupied space next to him.

"Thanks."

"Is that you?" he asked, picking up a photo of her and Nikki that was on a small table by his leg.

"Yes, don't," she said, leaning over and taking the picture from his hand.

He paused, looking at his empty hands. "She's a pretty girl." They made eye contact. "Is that who you were visiting the other day?"

The question was so gentle that it shook her.

"Yes, but I don't want to talk about it."

He shrugged, and she looked away. "Well, it's a beautiful picture of the two of you, anyway." He absently stroked the back of the couch, taking in the room.

Every once in a while Mia found him looking curiously at the photo, and she let her eyes gravitate there, too.

Her daughter's smiling face brought back every aspect of that day. She remembered how long it took to comb Nikki's

hair and convince her to wear the blue sailor dress, and how
Nikki had waited patiently while she changed her clothes again.

It had been grueling, getting to the photographer on time,
but worth it. That photo was the only formal picture she had
of them together.

"Your hair was longer," he noted. "It makes you look
softer," he said, breaking the silence.

"You don't have to say that. I was so big here," she said
plainly, and looked once more into their preserved faces.

Adam moved down the couch until he was next to her chair.
He touched the edge of the wooden frame. "Some photogra-
phers are good at capturing what's right in front of them." His
voice caressed her. "While others are good at preserving what
can't be seen on the surface. You're happy here. Your smile
is wide, your eyes sparkle, and she seems to be mischievous
and delightful. I could be wrong, but that's what I see when I
look at this."

Covering her disbelief at his accuracy, she replied sarcastically. "Yeah. Right," and stood.

She laid the picture flat on the counter and paced.

"I should be thanking you for the other night, and apologiz-
ing for today. Sorry."

"I don't accept," he said.

Her surprised gaze swung to his. He crossed the space with
two long strides and stood beside her.

Mia moved to the couch, but didn't sit down. "Why?"

He was right behind her, and his touch burned her hand.

His hold kept her from running, but it didn't stop her heart
from clamoring all over her chest.

"I'd like to take you to dinner as a peace offering."

"You don't have to do that. I was wrong and you were r-
right," she stuttered, eliciting a smile from his generous lips.

She focused on his hands, on how warm they were on her
arm. These strong hands had helped ease her suffering. They
held her when she needed assurance that she would live past

one moment to the next, and when she did they still supported her until the next.

Mia fought the growing feeling of attraction. She didn't need a man in her life. Any man.

She withdrew her arms from his grasp. She picked up a throw pillow and held it in front of her as if it would stop the attraction beam she felt flowing between them.

"I hope I'm not giving you the wrong impression, but I don't date."

"I'm sorry to hear that," he said, and didn't blink an eye at her declaration. "Do you have my suit coat?"

"Your suit coat!" she exclaimed. "Wait here. I'll get it." She threw the pillow down and was back a few seconds later, holding it against herself. "Here it is. I admit that I looked through your wallet to see if a number was there, but I didn't see one, so I put everything back, and it might not be in the right order, but you can check.

"The same two hundred dollars that was there, is still there." She inhaled, breathless from her babbling. "Nothing is missing."

Adam took the wrinkled coat and hung it on the front door-knob. He inserted his wallet in the breast pocket of the jacket he wore. "I didn't think there would be. Just a second," he said softly to stop her from moving away from him. "I want you to tell me something."

His eyes raked her from head to foot, and Mia crossed her arms over her chest, burning from the close scrutiny.

"Tell me you don't think I'm a pervert."

Mia got lost in the depth of his gaze. Her tongue darted out to moisten her lips, then she pressed them together. Clearing her throat, she glanced back at him to find him waiting.

"I—" She shrugged. "I don't think you're a pervert. I'm sorry about saying that. I was just angry—"

"And scared?" he added when she bit off the next words.

"Maybe," she said, lifting her chin, putting distance between them.

Jon and Star walked in at that moment. "Did we come back at a good time?" Star asked, her eyes volleying between them.

"Yes."

"No."

They answered in unison. Mia moved around Adam and cleared the picture and flowers off the small counter.

"How's everything going, girl?" Star asked. She flipped the lid on the pizza box and rolled cheese into a ball before popping it in her mouth.

"Fine," Mia said, and watched her massacre the face of the pizza slice, then throw the crust away. She reached for another, and Mia moved the box away.

"Quit. The rest of us might want some that you haven't drooled over." She spoke in hushed tones. "I'm dying for this night to be over."

She glanced at Adam, who was talking quietly with Jon. She wanted to tell him to stop looking so good, stop smelling so good, and stop breathing her air. But she couldn't. She wouldn't.

"Do you think they're talking about us?" Mia asked, eyeing them suspiciously. She dropped hot pizza slices on plates.

"No," Star replied with a grin on her face. "They're talking about you. Dinner," she called and walked out of the kitchen.

Mia had never laughed so hard in her life. Jon and Star were amateur comedians, and she and Adam were their captive audience. Throughout the evening he couldn't seem to help touching her. On the surface, the touches were innocent enough, but underneath lay a molten stream. There were soft caresses and lingering looks and intimate smiles. Not something two strangers shared.

Once, he even wiped wine off her leg that he accidentally spilled while laughing at J.R.'s impressions of Esther doing aerobics. Another time, he touched the tip of his nose and pointed to her.

She looked down, cross-eyed, but before she could swipe at

it he reached out and relieved her of an offending piece of tomato. Every touch was a hint of something private, something seductive. It excited and scared her.

Playing cards wasn't much better. They kept losing, and Adam kept having strategy huddles. He draped his arm over her shoulder and bent over at the waist, reviewing the plan. So what if his touch burned through her sweatshirt? She couldn't focus. They lost again.

Now he was calling for another.

"Come here, partner. We need a huddle." They walked to the closet, and he companionably put his arm over her shoulder again. *Good grief.* "How are you at gin?" he asked.

When she waved her hand in the air he shrugged. "Those are better odds than we have right now." He glanced over his shoulder, then drew her nearer.

"I'm tired of losing. How about you?"

She would have agreed to anything he said. "Yeah, me too," she moaned.

"Just keep your eye on me." He winked. "Let's go kick some butt."

Mia was delighted when they started winning. Adam gave her encouraging winks, even a high five when she got ten spades and took over the game. His competitive energy rubbed off on her, and she reveled in it.

Star threw her cards in after the fifth game, yawning.

"I've had it. I think it's a conspiracy to overthrow us. J.R.?"

Mia giggled when he fell back on the floor and pretended to snore. "Jon, it's time to go home."

"I'm up," he said, snoring again.

"Why do you call him Jon?" Adam asked.

"I just haven't gotten in the habit of calling him J.R. He keeps telling me to, but . . ." She shrugged. "I guess I can."

"J.R., Star, I need a private moment with Mia."

Silence fell. Mia began to tingle and the cards slid from her hands.

"Again?" J.R. groaned. "First we can't stop them from

wanting to kill each other and now we can't stop them from talking privately. Come on, baby, and let's go make out in the car.''

Star gave Mia a hug and Adam the thumbs up.

''I had a good time tonight,'' he said, helping her straighten up once the door had closed behind Jon and Star.

''So did I.''

He paused and palmed the deck of cards. ''So, will you go out with me?''

Mia shook her head, her smile fading. ''I don't want to give you the wrong impression.''

''What impression would that be? You don't snort. I've heard you laugh. You don't have an unpleasant odor. I've enjoyed smelling you all night.''

Despite herself, she smiled.

''Ah, and the most compelling reason is that you think I'm funny.''

Mia tried to control the grin tugging at the corners of her lips, but couldn't. ''I don't know,'' she said, a note of question in her voice.

''Well then, we won't call it a date. You have to eat, don't you?'' She nodded, rubbing her arms. ''Well then, it can be an I'm hungry, you're hungry, mutual chewing thing, but not a date. How's that?'' He lifted his eyebrows at the novel approach, his eyes reflecting his amusement.

Mia smiled noncommittally, then nodded.

He picked up his wrinkled jacket and opened the front door. He turned on the porch, his eyes lingering on her.

''You're very pretty when you cry.'' Mia felt her breath catch. ''But you're exquisite when you smile.''

She watched as he walked down the stairs and folded his long frame in the back seat of Star's car.

Chapter 4

Mia tried to stop fidgeting while waiting for Adam to walk through the door of her apartment. She couldn't help herself.

One part of her was excited that she was going to see him again. He was a handsome, available man who seemed genuinely interested in her. But another side of her was riddled with doubt. Was his interest just morbid curiosity? Especially after how they met? She aimed to find out.

Mia opened the door and was greeted with dark purple blooms. Enclosed in a round glass dish, the beautiful roses halted the question she was ready to fire at him.

"Y—you caught me off guard," she said breathlessly.

A smile upturned his generous lips.

"Let's go. You can tell me about it on the way."

Before Mia could catch her breath Adam had taken her keys from her hand and locked the door. They were in the car and on the highway within minutes.

The black Jeep hugged the road and gave a smooth ride. Mia still sat erect, with her hand firmly on the door handle.

"Do you ever relax?"

"Of course," she said, slightly indignant, releasing the door to prove her point.

"Okay, then what do you do for fun?"

"Plenty of things," she answered, hoping he wouldn't ask what.

"Like what?"

"Why?"

"I'm curious to know what makes you laugh. But since you won't tell me," his lingering gaze stopped on her lips, "then I thought tonight we would have fun Webster style."

She sat forward in the seat.

"What's that?"

He stroked her arm and didn't try to hide the amusement in his voice. "We're not going to any strip clubs or anything, so wipe that look off your face."

She hadn't realized he could see her features so well in the darkness of the Jeep. But she could surely see his. And from her observation, he had the longest, darkest eyelashes she had ever seen on a man. Mia dragged her eyes away from them and stared at the taillights of the car in front of them. That was much safer. "Where exactly are we going?" she asked, unfamiliar with the area they were in.

"It's top secret," he said mysteriously. "You're guaranteed to enjoy it, or come to me for a full refund."

They exited the highway and stopped at the light.

Her knee jumped and Mia crossed her legs at the ankle, trying to control the nervous shaking.

"I hope I'm dressed all right," she mumbled.

She was aware of Adam's eyes making their way down her body. The darkness of the Jeep was sequestering, and she felt like she was on private display.

For his eyes only. A pleasant heat thread through her veins, and she grew flushed from his appreciative gaze.

He started at her hair, and seemed to glide through every curl and twist, then moved down her long graceful neck. She felt his eyes linger on the tops of her bare shoulders, and her heart hammered when they passed over the curve of her breasts.

Mia held her breath as he finished his perusal and looked up just as he did.

When his eyes locked with hers, she felt a strong wave of attraction she hadn't felt in a long time. She sat back and kept quiet when he took off from the light and drove through downtown and past the Atlanta airport.

Cool jazz floated through the car as they headed south on the long, busy street. "You don't sound like a native," she said, breaking the silence. "Are you from here?"

"No."

"How did you come to live here?"

"After my father died in a car crash when I was a boy, my mother and I decided to move here."

"Oh, I'm sorry."

"It was a long time ago," he said quietly, but she saw a lingering sadness in his dark eyes.

"What do you do, Adam?"

"Why do you say it like that?"

"I just wondered. You know so much about roses, I thought maybe you do more than work with plants."

She was rewarded with a smile.

"I have a master's degree in horticulture, and I own a couple of wholesale companies. One of my specialties is roses. How about you? First, where are you from? And then you can tell me what you did before you became an aerobics instructor."

"I'm from the home of the Bulls. That's the Chicago Bulls." Her eyebrow arched, and a light challenge laced her voice.

"You know the Bulls aren't going to win another championship," he teased.

"Oh, please. As long as there's basketball, the Bulls will at least make it to the playoffs."

"What else?" he questioned gently.

"There's not much else to tell. I moved here several years ago and now I'm an aerobics instructor."

Mia couldn't help being evasive. She rarely talked about her past. The few times she had, it made people feel it was okay to comment on her life, and she wasn't down for that.

"Something must have dragged you from that fine blistering cold," Adam probed.

"I got a job here," she said, gazing out the window at the bright stars. Mia held on as he U-turned in the street and pulled into a poorly lit parking lot.

"Where are your folks? Still in Chicago?"

"Yes," she said, wanting to end the subject of her past.

"Brothers or sisters?"

"Why do you want to know so much about me? You sound like you're compiling data for the U.S. Census." Mia paused after her outburst, then touched his arm apologetically. "I'm sorry. You don't deserve that. I don't have any brothers or sisters. No cousins, either. I do have friends and coll—" She ended the sentence abruptly.

The Jeep seemed to grow smaller as they sat within its dark cozy confines.

"What were you going to say, college buddies?"

Mia licked her lips, debating whether she should tell him the truth or not.

"No, colleagues. I'm a pediatrician."

"What did you say?"

Mia was accustomed to this reaction, and, frankly, she was tired of it. She could do whatever she wanted to with her life, and that was that.

"I said, pediatrician. Do you have a problem with that?"

"Not if you don't. I'm sure when the time is right, you'll tell me about it."

He leaned closer and closer, and she wondered what he was about to do. He extended his right arm in front of her.

"Don't kiss me!"

Click.

Cool wind rushed up her back as the passenger door swung open. "I could have opened it myself," she said in a small, defensive voice. She fumbled with the straps of her bag. He hadn't even commented on one thing she'd said. It was as if it didn't matter to him. In a way, she wanted to know what he thought.

Mia stepped out of the car and lingered under his intense gaze. They walked to the door, and when she held back he draped his arm around her waist and drew her near. It was a friendly gesture, but she felt a more-than-friendly rush from his touch.

Their eyes locked, and her heart pounded against her chest. "You don't want to leave, do you?"

She shook her head.

"Then, let's go in."

Morgan's wasn't a disappointment.

Adam was glad he had chosen it. The food was good and the atmosphere private and intimate.

The more time he spent with Mia, the bigger the mystery. She was a pediatrician turned aerobic instructor. What had happened? The question lingered in his mind, but he didn't want to scare her by probing too much.

Adam kept her hand within his and gave his name to the hostess.

He caught himself staring at her lips, and he wondered how long it would be before he couldn't resist kissing them.

Adam shifted his thoughts to something safe.

He had learned so much about her their first night together. She liked Chinese food, and jazz. She wasn't married, and he was grateful to hear that. She had an interesting philosophy on why she didn't date, but whenever he tried to probe deeper she grew quiet, almost sad.

He hadn't met a woman who never wanted to talk about herself. But here was Mia, her life full of secrets and ghosts, wanting to keep it all hidden. What could be so bad?

He couldn't figure it, but he knew he would find out.

"Adam, this place is wonderful." Her eyes rolled heavenward as a platter of ribs and macaroni and cheese passed under her nose. He gave his name to the hostess and they waited in front for a table.

He wrapped his arms around her waist, playfully pulling her back. "Makes your mouth water, doesn't it?"

Two diamonds sparkled in her ear as they backed up, allowing another couple to pass.

Her back stiffened, then her body relaxed against his. It felt comfortable and right.

She turned slightly, still locked in his arms, and spoke, her breath fanning across his face.

"Adam, they called our name," she said, looking at him.

"What did they say?" he said absently, too preoccupied with controlling his urge to kiss her.

"Webster," she answered, confused.

"Then let's not keep them waiting," he said, snapping out of it.

Mia looked gorgeous. Against the backdrop of deep blues, gold, and candlelight, she made it all intimate and elegant. The menus lay on the table, and she raised her eyes, oblivious to his perusal.

"Your hair is gorgeous. What did you do to it?"

"Oh, this is compliments of Star. She came over to see what I was wearing tonight. She did some kind of new curl thing. I don't know how she knows all these things. But I chose the clothes."

"I like the clothes."

When she looked away in embarrassment, he laughed and snapped his menu open. The waiter returned at his signal, and he placed a wine order. The flickering candle made her eyes luminescent, and he was attracted like a moth to a flame.

"What would you like to eat?"

Her mouth formed a zero, then she tickled her ear. "Everything looks good. Why don't you order for me?" Adam perused the menu and ordered them both a full rack of ribs. He winked at her and she blushed.

"You're very sensitive," he said, once the waiter was gone. "You blush at a wink, you're embarrassed when I compliment you. I'd hate to see what you'd do if I kissed you."

"Don't." She shook her head, resting her arms on the table.

"May I ask why?"

Her expression grew serious. She sat up in the chair and was suddenly tense. Unable to stop the impulse, he reached over and stroked the base of her jaw.

"You don't have to worry about me. I'll let you decide when you want to be kissed, or held or touched."

Their food arrived, and regretfully he let his hand slip from her face. It didn't stop him from admiring her gracefulness, and the delicate way she tried to cut her ribs off the bone. Nor was he able to stop laughing when she threw the fork on the table and picked up the bones with her fingers and sank her teeth in them.

Adam watched her wrap her lips around the succulent meat. Her tongue darted out, licking sauce from the sides of her mouth, and she closed her eyes with a moan.

She drew the bone from her lips and dropped it onto her plate, picking up another. "These are good. You don't like yours?"

He hadn't realized that he'd stopped eating. It could have been sawdust, for all he cared. Just then her foot touched his and he jerked, his long legs bumping the table.

"Sorry."

"It was nothing," he managed to choke out. He didn't know how long it would be before he sought relief in the form of tasting her succulent mouth.

Adam swallowed some wine and she continued to eat, oblivious to his lack of interest in his food. When their plates were cleared away, he felt comfortable asking her about her life.

"What made you leave medicine?"

Mia spun her glass in a slow circle, staring into the red liquid. "I didn't decide overnight. My life changed, and I didn't feel

I could deal with the demands of the job anymore. So I took a two year leave of absence."

"Do you think you'll ever return?"

She shook her head and shrugged. "I don't know."

"So," he joked. "If I were choking to death you could still save me, right?"

"You're bigger than the average newborn, so I guess that would call for extreme measures." She looked him over and nodded reassuringly. "I think I could manage to hoist you over my shoulder and pat you on the back."

They both laughed, enjoying the moment. Then she grew serious. "I haven't forgotten how to do my job. I think about it sometimes. I take the required courses each year to keep up." Her shoulders slumped. "Maybe if Nikki had lived . . ." Her startled gaze swung to his, and she folded her napkin, sitting straight in her chair.

"How did it happen?" He inched his chair close to hers so that they sat side by side. Their table was in the back, and they had complete privacy.

Loneliness seemed to surround her, and he touched her back in a soft caress. The pain fully enveloped her like a blinding fog.

"If it's too difficult . . ."

"No. I can talk about it." She took a strengthening breath. "Nikki was only two years old, and somehow she got outside, into the pool, and drowned."

"Mia," he said softly.

She brushed aside his offer of comfort. "I'm okay. Actually, when you saw me the other day that was the first time I had been out there in two years. It was difficult knowing she was there."

"You shouldn't have gone by yourself," he said, knowing the power of grieving alone. It could be overwhelming. "Next time you need a friend you call me, okay?"

"Thanks, I'll keep that in mind." Her manner made clear her opinion. She would never call him.

Mia crossed her legs, then shifted, crossing them again, trying to emotionally distance herself from him.

It was obvious she hadn't meant to reveal so much about herself, and she struggled with it. She avoided contact with him, and when he touched her hand she drew it back as if she were burned.

"Who were you out there to see?" she asked, the firelight playing with the shadow behind her.

"My mother," he answered softly. For the first time, she stared deep into his eyes. What she did next pleasantly surprised him.

She hugged him.

How did it happen?" she asked, drawing away from him but leaving her arm on his chair.

"Hodgkin's disease. Four months ago."

"I'm sorry." Her hand covered his, and he accepted her show of support. She couldn't take help for herself, but she could give it to someone. Mia kept surprising him.

"You're all alone, too? No brothers or sisters?"

He shook his head and shrugged.

"I'm very lucky. I have J.R. and Pops. They love me like I was blood."

Adam motioned for the check. He gave the waiter his credit card and waited for him to walk away.

Distantly, he could hear the sounds of the restaurant behind him. The clinking of silverware and glasses. Even the music he had never noticed before. But each sound slipped away when she lowered her head and her eyes glistened. Against the candlelight she looked beautiful and sad.

"Mia, where do you go when you need love?"

He touched her provocative curls and wanted to lose his fingers in the thickness of her hair. The swept-up style showed off her long neck and accented the smoothness of her dark skin. The white blouse contrasted with her dark complexion, and he wouldn't have minded holding her again.

"I don't go anywhere. I don't need love," she whispered.

Her clear polished fingernails were the only thing he dared to touch as they fluttered against her earlobe.

Adam drew them to his lips, letting his kiss linger. When he drew them away, he helped her stand. His arms slid around her with a naturalness that was comfortable.

"Everybody needs love, from the bum on the street, to the richest person in the world. It's not something you can buy, but something the right person has to bring out of you." He tilted her chin slightly back until her raised eyes met his. "You're worthy of love. I only hope that I get to be the one who shows you what's inside you."

"You don't know me," she said, and shifted as if she were ready to be let go.

He snuggled her closer and smiled. "You're right, I don't. But I want to. You're attractive and you have a quick temper." Her heart beat faster and he couldn't let her go. "But you can also be sympathetic and admit when you're wrong and I'm right," he teased, and wriggled a smile out of her.

His eyes grew serious, touched with flames of desire.

"I want us to get to know one another better. One of these days, you're going to have to take a chance." He traced the shell of her ear, then kissed it softly. Then he stepped back and released her. "So, it's up to you. Do you still want to have fun tonight?"

Time slowed to a drag as he waited for her answer. He read the uncertainty and distrust in her eyes, and yearned to reassure her that he would never hurt her. But words wouldn't help. Whatever bothered her went too deep. She had to be shown.

"I—uh." Her hoarse whisper grated his eardrum, and he resisted taking her back into his arms.

"I'm not that wolf in sheep's clothes. What you see, is what there is. So, what's it going to be? Do we continue our evening of fun, not knowing where it will take us, or do I drop you off and we say goodbye forever?"

Chapter 5

Mia couldn't deny that she found Adam attractive. She couldn't explain why, but whenever she was in his company she wanted to smile. Or that whenever he looked at her, she became aware of the power of her femininity.

She cocked her head to the side and looked up into his dark eyes. They weren't unusual in color, but they still caught her off guard. For the past two years, she had rarely looked anyone in the eye. The warmth and confidence in them made her decide quickly.

"What kind of fun did you have in mind?" she asked, feigning casualness.

"Tell me first if you want to go with me," he said evenly. "I don't want you to feel that I'm forcing you into something you don't want to do. But be assured," his voice lowered seductively, "you won't be disappointed."

The slide of the back of his fingers down her face sent fireworks shooting through her body. The tingle turned into a slow burn, and Mia meant to turn her cheek away from the sweet torture. She wondered for a moment if the rest of her body would burn this way from his experienced hands. The flickering candlelight surrounding them lent intimacy to the silken touch, and she moved closer. She lifted her cheek from his hand and spoke around the thundering of her heart.

"I want to go."

"Good," he said, his tone deep, tortuous, and promising.

Her hand fit snugly into his larger one, and they left the restaurant and climbed into the car. The ride lasted less than twenty minutes before they stopped in the heart of downtown Atlanta.

Mia looked around suspiciously at the dark alley parking, and didn't budge. Adam unbuckled his seat belt and had his hand on the door before he noticed that she hadn't moved.

"What's the matter?" he asked, noticing her staid expression.

"We're going in there?"

He gave her a devilishly handsome grin. "Yes. Is there a problem?"

"What kind of place is this?" Mia hated the way her voice shook, but the place looked too dark for there to be anything going on inside that she would be interested in.

He laughed. "It's a place where people go dancing."

Adam opened the door and the warning bells from the car started to ding. Mia felt the same warning ring within herself.

"But I can't—," she said, and heaved an exasperated sigh when he closed the car door. "Adam, I can't dance," she said when he opened her door and helped her out.

"Well, tonight, you will," he said with a confident smile, and took her hand again.

The plain black building looked ominous from the outside. A single door opened to a hallway, and once inside they were surrounded by surveillance cameras, metal detectors and tough looking guards who blocked more doors.

After passing each safety point and paying the cover charge, they were escorted through two additional black doors.

Rhythmic rap music pulsated around them. They wove their way through the packed room and stopped briefly at the bottom of some wide stairs to look over their shoulders.

"We just passed through a generation gap," Adam said, placing his hand on her back, urging her up the stairs.

Following the bright indicator lights, they walked down a long hallway toward music that was slower and comfortably familiar. Songs popular from the eighties blasted from huge speakers, and they turned to each other and nodded in silent agreement. This was the place for them.

"Come on, let's dance," he said, taking her hand. She held back. "Adam, I can't dance. I told you I can't dance," she repeated, steadily backing further into the crowd.

"Even if you can't dance, anything you do is going to look good to me. You're an aerobics instructor—improvise."

He guided her into the center of the dance floor, moving his body to the beat.

Mia shoved her hand in her pocket and watched the people around her. They danced so provocatively. There was no way she was going to be able to come close to their undulations. She frowned, watching one couple. Had their clothes been off, who knew what would have happened?

"Are you this stubborn about everything, woman?" Adam growled in her ear, reaching for her. His large hands gently captured her waist, and he smoothly twisted her towards him.

She still didn't dance.

He hadn't released her when he said, "If you're going to let me do this, I'd rather be somewhere else."

His hands moved swiftly across her hips, lightly coming to rest on her backside. He moved close, anticipating her jump of surprise so that their bodies were flush against each other.

Flustered by the shock of his bold action and the pleasurable sensations his hands elicited from her, Mia stumbled, then held onto his arms, smiling despite herself.

He was determined, and so was she. She was going to have fun.

"Okay, I'll dance," she said, and turned her attention to the other dancers. But the best instructor stood before her. Adam moved so smoothly that several times Mia had to drag her eyes away from places she shouldn't have been looking. But they gravitated, and she let them wander.

She loosened up, letting the music carry her through the night until she lost count of the number of songs they danced to.

Catching him looking at her, she wondered what he was thinking. "What are you smiling at? Am I that bad?"

"You're that good."

"You're not so bad, yourself," she said easily.

An old tune, "You and I", blasted through the five hundred-watt speakers, and the floor became packed with dancers. She stepped closer to Adam and tried to direct her gaze away from the curling hairs on his chest that were visible beneath his Adam's apple.

His denim shirt hugged his chest, and she searched, trying to find another resting place for her eyes.

Nothing is going to come from this, she reminded herself. It might be a date, but there can't be a second.

Mia slowed and looked around, feeling as if she didn't belong there.

"I'm tired," she said, and began to walk through the crowd. His hands gripped her on either side of her waist. Turning her, he swept her close and laced his fingers through hers, raising them to his lips.

"Adam, don't," she said sharply, her hand on fire from the smooth tease of his lips. Conflicting emotions tore through her. Jostled by the gyrating couple next to them, Mia was pushed back against him. "Sorry," the guy mumbled, and he continued his convulsive dance.

Adam's arms automatically reached out to her, and she looked up.

"I overreacted again," she whispered, unable to mask wanting to be in his arms.

The romantic sounds of the clarinet worked like a snake charmer's flute as its woodwind sound hypnotized her.

Johnny Gill's tune "My, My, My," echoed from the speakers, and she dared her mouth to speak what her heart cried for. Inching up on her toes, she said, "Dance with me, please?"

He didn't speak, just guided her closer until their bodies molded together like two interlocking puzzle pieces.

She moved cautiously at first, then couldn't resist the urge to close her eyes. The people surrounding them disappeared, and she gave herself to the music, to their sensual rhythm. It was so easy. He held her as if he'd never let her go.

Repressed desire welled within her, and she yielded to the symphony of urgings. Mia locked her arms around his neck, pulling his head down beside hers.

Her lips touched his cheek and she ran her hand over his shoulders and back, loving the feel of him against her.

Adam growled deep in his chest and gripped her hips, his thigh capturing hers as they ground to the music.

His arousal pressed into her center. A moan escaped her lips, plunging her back into reality.

Mia broke the spell, stepping unsteadily out of his arms. "Can we leave?" she croaked, her throat dry.

"Are you sure you're ready?" She caught the hidden meaning in his question.

If she didn't stop now, there would be no never. She nodded. "Let's go."

The drive on the highway was quiet while Mia tried to gain some perspective on the evening.

Her body still hummed a desirous tune, as if she had received a transfusion. He's only a man. *A man who could make me forget,* she thought, sneaking a glance at him. But he didn't seem to want just that. He wanted to talk about it, and talking led to acceptance. She wasn't ready for that quite yet.

The lights of her apartment building glowed ahead and Adam braked the Jeep beside her car.

Too close, too soon. She rambled nervously. "I can't find my keys. I know I put them somewhere. Oh, that's right, you have them."

Her knee jumped from nervousness, and her hand slammed down on it. She looked at his lips and started to shake.

I'm not kissing him!

Mia stuck her hand out, then withdrew it. The silence was deafening. *Why doesn't he say something? Instead of letting me make a fool of myself?* Sticking out her hand again, she broke the lengthy silence.

"Th—thank you, Adam. I had a great time." Her voice grew husky while she waited for his touch.

It never came.

He merely smiled and opened his door, then hers.

He gave nothing away as they walked up the stairs to her door.

"Thank you, Adam," she said again.

Their gazes collided, and Mia immediately knew looking into the smoky depths of his eyes was a mistake.

"What are you doing?" she whispered hoarsely, blinking quickly, resisting his touch, yet knowing it was inevitable.

"Something I've wanted to do all night. Since I can't kiss you . . . well, I have to do the next best thing."

"Adam . . ."

Her voice caught as his hand cupped her jaw, tilting it sideways. His face came closer, his breath fanning across her cheek, past her lips.

A tickle from his forefinger shot straight to her toes, then to her hair roots, leaving her shivering with unfamiliar desire.

He tilted her face further back. Then . . .

Contact.

Hot and cool. Soft, yet demanding, gentle lips.

It took a moment before she realized what the sweet, sensational torture was.

He was sucking her face.

Her body tensed, then her knees gave out as she collapsed into his chest, her arms connecting around his waist, holding on. His body anchored her against the door. Otherwise, she undoubtedly she would have fallen.

Mia knew the penalty for the intense pleasure.

Complete surrender.

She felt all vestiges of control slide away. Her moans of pleasure echoed loudly in the night. Her fingers slid beneath the vest to touch his heated back.

"Adam . . . please," she begged, wanting him to stop yet unable to resist the pleasure he created.

"Do you want me to stop?" he asked around her chin, finding a resting place on the large expanse of flesh on her neck.

She exhaled. "I . . . don't . . . know."

"Delicious . . . you taste so good," he groaned seconds later, tasting her earlobe.

"Enough!"

Mia braced her hands on his shoulders, pushing him away. She fumbled in her purse, looking for her keys, needing to be away from him. Her own behavior was too disturbing to fathom. She could only blame Adam for the change.

He stepped alongside her, unlocked the door, cut on the light, and checked the tiny apartment.

Reassured, he stepped back outside and placed the key in her outstretched hand.

"Aren't you going in?" he asked, cocking a dark eyebrow at her.

"Yes." To prove her point she stepped over the threshold. "I just wanted you out before I went in," she retorted.

Gently he cupped her chin. She stopped breathing, while the pad of his thumb activated the tender spot, urging it to respond to his touch. "Goodnight. See you tomorrow."

Speechless, she stepped back and slammed the door.

Mia stamped around the room, talking as she undressed.

"Who does he think *he* is? How can he do this to *me?* I was fine until I met him. Now I'm hanging out in clubs, and getting nasty on my own front steps. I must be losing my everloving mind."

Don't trust him, she told herself continually.

Mia sighed and sat down on the bed. Absently she hung her legs over the side, shaking them.

What would a virile, healthy man like Adam Webster want with me? she wondered. A jolt shot through her, and she burned, remembering how thick his desire felt pressing into her.

I can't do that.

Self-defeating thoughts besieged her, and she leaned back and closed her eyes.

This won't go anywhere. A relationship with him can't happen. She got off the bed and pulled on her pajamas, throwing her clothes in the hamper.

She spread a generous amount of toothpaste on her toothbrush and lifted her hand to her teeth. The toothbrush clamored into the sink.

The telltale marks of a hickey practically shouted from her neck, ''Adam Webster has been here!''

Her body seemed to awaken as she touched the spot where his lips had been making love to her. It responded as if he were there working his special magic. She snatched up the toothbrush and brushed furiously, remembering every single place his body had touched hers.

Mia scrubbed her teeth harder, until she was sure there wasn't any enamel. She rinsed the toothbrush, her eyes stuck like glue to the purple spot on her neck.

Tonight was a big mistake, and it won't happen again, she vowed, climbing into the bed and punching the pillow into a comfortable position.

So that was fun Webster style, she thought, long after she was supposed to be asleep. His lips on her face, the five o'clock shadow that scraped her cheek, and his strong arms holding her against him.

She took those images with her into her dreams when she finally slept, late, late that night.

Chapter 6

Distant pink dawn eclipsed the night sky, the promise of a beautiful day peeking through the clouds.

Panting set the rhythm of his run as Adam jogged the last two miles in record time. Refreshed and calmer after his restless night alone in bed, he felt the pressure and desire he had otherwise been unable to shake since meeting Mia ease.

Turning up the winding lane to the four bedroom house he now called home, Adam was struck again by the serene beauty of the place. Built like a miniature mansion, the brick wraparound had been Grace Webster's pride and joy.

White pillars lined the front of the elegant home that spoke so much about his mother. It was a lively place with ivy running up the west and east walls and manicured evergreen bushes growing in abundance along the front.

She had worked closely with the builder, designing the master suite and private living area on the second level.

Two stories high and five thousand square feet, the main house was decorated with understated elegance that every guest found inviting and comforting. The rooms were bright and airy.

Since Adam had moved back six months ago, he had been

in constant turmoil over whether to keep the house or sell it to a family who would fill it with people and love.

Planned as her legacy to him, it had been fully paid off after her death, so he wouldn't have to struggle as much as she and his father did when they began their lives together.

Jogging up the lane, he spotted a small red sports car sitting in the middle of the winding driveway. Shaking his head, he groaned, knowing the morning had immediately taken a turn for the worse.

Sleek with perspiration, Adam ran the final steps up the drive as the sun crested the horizon, bathing his bronze skin in warmth.

Opening the front door, Adam passed Candice Walker, his former girlfriend, without comment, knowing she would follow.

"Adam," she called, enunciating every syllable of his name. "Your secretary is an incompetent, old, rude, bag of waste. I don't know why you keep her."

The taps on her Italian-made designer shoes clicked in precise, measured steps as she followed his jogging body into the kitchen.

"I know she hasn't given you my messages. You should get rid of her and find someone from this past half-century to work for you." She spoke to his sweating back as he bent low at the refrigerator.

Retrieving the water bottle, he tipped it up and drank thirstily from it before turning to stare at her. From head to toe, Candice reminded him of a porcelain doll, beautiful on the outside, but her heart was made of glass.

Her hair was always perfectly coiffed, and not one bit of makeup was ever out of place. She was petite, but moved with the velocity of a tornado when she didn't get her way, and she was churning now.

She watched him drink, a disgusted expression on her face. Flicking unseen lint from her jacket, Candice pulled herself to her full height of five foot, four inches in heels and tapped her manicured fingernails on the marble countertop.

"I know you're trying to irritate me, but I'll forgive you. Why haven't you called?" Her question demanded an answer.

"Yes, she has."

"Adam, keep up. I asked you a question." Irritated, she fluttered her hand in the air, dismissing the jug he thrust in her direction.

"I'm answering your question. Yes. Angela has given me your messages. I've chosen not to answer them. We don't have any more to say to each other. As in, I don't owe you a phone call, because I don't want to talk to you. Clear enough?"

Mouth agape, Candice stared at him, her face molten with anger. She quickly smoothed the angry lines away and walked suggestively toward him.

"Adam, enough time has passed that you can forgive me. I was under immense pressure." Her sigh was supposed to elicit a response from him. It didn't.

"We were supposed to be getting engaged," she hurried on. "How was I to know your mother was going to take a turn for the worse? She had been sick so long. I just figured we would go on with our plans."

Adam grew tired of her charade. "Candice, we didn't have any plans. We were through long before my mother died."

He looked at the woman he once thought he loved, and his eyes narrowed. "You know what ended it? I don't think you really know."

Adam banged the jug of water on the counter. "Your manipulative lie. You knew that I wanted a family, and you used that to try to stop our breakup. For a whole month you let me walk around thinking I was going to be a father." His voice was disgusted as he continued. "You faked a pregnancy to get what you wanted, then used the fact that my mother was dying to manipulate me."

He opened the refrigerator, then slammed it, fueled by his anger. "What kind of life together did you think we would have after that?"

"Okay," she spat, her face creasing into an ugly grimace.

"Telling you I was pregnant wasn't the most original idea. But I didn't know how else to get your attention."

She walked up to him and minced no words. "You and I are perfect together. We're both ambitious, driven people. No, I don't want to play in dirt all day like you, and I'm sure as hell not going to stand behind a counter and wait on people in one of my father's godforsaken stores."

Adam laughed with genuine humor. Her attitude would have him out of business in twenty-four hours.

She continued, ignoring his mirthless smile. "We could build Walker's Floral Shops into a dynasty. With your wholesale business and me by your side." Her eyes gleamed. "We could be rich."

He shook his head, unable to believe what he was hearing.

"You and I are through, Candice," he said in the most basic tone he could use to make her understand.

"There is no going back. Do you get it? We're done. You have no feelings in your body for anyone but yourself. We were over long before you lied to me about the baby. Sometimes it surprises me that I once thought I loved you." Adam shook his head, his voice grim.

"Love? What's that?" Her harsh laughter marred her perfect features. "Remember me, Adam? Candice Walker? Walker's Flower Shops? My family can put Webster's Wholesalers on the map or blast them off. I'm no fool. You need me for all your big dreams to come true, and I need you for mine."

She picked up her beige clutch purse and crisply clipped it under her arm.

"I'm not above lying to get what I want. My father will be very disappointed to hear that you forced me into having an abortion, taking his first grandchild's life."

Adam had heard enough. He clenched his teeth and took hold of her arm, firmly escorting her to the front door. If she stayed any longer, he was sure he wouldn't be able to control his murderous thoughts.

"You won't do it, Candice. Get out, now."

Her voice stopped him cold. "What have I got to lose, Adam? According to the terms of my trust, I have to have a degree or be employed by my twenty-eighth birthday before I can receive any of my money. I have neither of those. Or I have to be married." Her eyes narrowed. "I can't just marry *anybody,*" she emphasized. "I choose you."

"I'm not part of your plot, Candice. I can't help you."

He released her arm after putting her on the front porch. In the sunlight, she resembled the picture of perfection. Only he could see the deep crack that cut down the front of her chest, with a huge space where her heart should have been.

Her heels clicked against the cement on the way to her car. Opening the car door, she slid into the bucket seat and leveled a warning look at him.

"I won't have regrets, Adam. You will."

The engine gunned to life, and with remarkable calmness she steered the car off the driveway and out of sight.

There was no doubt in his mind that Candice scorned was like a lion with a thorn. Trouble.

Adam picked up the phone and dialed Angela. Although he knew she would be in church at this hour, he decided to leave her a message on her recorder.

"Ange, Adam. Please prepare for me first thing in the morning a list of shops and stores we supply inventory to. Also, I want you to break out Walker's Flower Shops separately. I need it on my desk in the morning. One more thing before I hang up. Call an executive staff meeting for nine o'clock. I want everybody there except Yvonne from new accounts. We need to keep her working. Thanks, Angela," he said, hanging up, assured she would follow his instructions to the letter.

The phone rang immediately when he hung up.

"Hello?"

"Hey, man," J.R. said. "I'm planning a couple of b—ball games in the club after we close tonight. Are you in?"

Adam leaned back and rotated his shoulders, tension from several days ago returning. It sounded like just what he needed.

He sighed heavily. He had too much to do to prepare the house, to even consider selling it. Those plans would have to go on hold. His instincts told him to take Candice seriously.

"I can't today," he said finally. "I have planting to do in the garden, and I also need to get some work done."

He placed the phone on his other shoulder and walked up the winding staircase to his room. "I need to talk to you, anyway."

"We'll talk tonight," J.R. said convincingly. "Come on, man. We need your height."

"No," Adam said more forcefully than he planned.

"What's up?"

"It's a long story," Adam said. "Let me put you on the speaker phone."

"Am I on yet?" J.R. asked, his voice booming into the room.

"Yeah, big mouth. Wait a second." Adam adjusted the volume and sat down in front of the window, unlacing his shoes. He dropped the right, then worked on the laces of the left. "J.R., come by and hang out now while I take care of the garden."

"Man, are you trying to sucker me into replanting that garden again?" J.R. laughed, his voice bouncing off the walls. "Adam, I'm not buying your game this time."

Adam chuckled at the memory of how he tricked J.R. into helping him plant the one acre garden of flowers and vegetables, almost five years ago.

"I'm just replanting and fertilizing today. That's all. Be here at eleven o'clock." Hanging up the phone, Adam headed for the shower.

Chapter 7

"Mia, you pushed us too hard today," complained Scout Cooperman at the end of the high-impact aerobics class.

Stepping from the platform, Mia congenially threw her arm around the old man and squeezed quickly before releasing him.

"Too hard, come on," she teased, laughing when others groaned their collective displeasure. She dabbed the moisture from her face with her towel, becoming thoughtful. The group *did* have a limp, washed-out look about them.

Trying valiantly to sway someone to her side, she tried again. "I know you all hate quick step, but around-the-world isn't that bad." Quickly demonstrating the knee up, straddle, knee up maneuver, Mia garnered no supporters.

"Where's your sense of adventure? This was easy. Jen, Helen, did you think I was too hard today?" They nodded in agreement, and she did a mental check of the routine.

Having choreographed some difficult moves into the "high-impact" routine, she hadn't planned to use them until she worked out the kinks.

But when she had come into the club today, she had needed something to help alleviate her frustration.

She looked apologetically at the group and squeezed Helen's arm.

Helen caught her hand, her voice laced with wisdom. "The only thing that could get me all worked up like that when I was a young woman, was a man. Is there a special guy? If not, our son Josh is still available."

"Helen," Mia cut in, laughing, then quickly erased her smile under the woman's disapproving gaze. "Josh is nice, but I don't date." She ignored the hot rush she felt as a reminder of her actions from the previous evening. "Remember, I told you that when you tried to fix us up before." Focusing her attention on Scout, she turned her back to Helen, allowing no opportunity for more discussion.

"Scout, you look tired, and you're a little pale. How are you feeling?"

Mia eyed the older man. Without thinking, she took his pulse and checked his pupils. Abruptly, she stopped as if she'd been burned.

"Mia, he's been feeling terrible since yesterday. I told him not to take the class today, but what do I know? We've only been married thirty-seven years, and I don't know fatigue when I see it." Helen's nasal voice grated in her ears.

Mia laid her palm against his forehead, the skin cool and clammy to the touch. He swore under his breath, shaking her off.

"Shut up, old lady. First you offer this wonderful girl our son, who's a lazy slob. Even if she were Jewish, I wouldn't allow him to marry her."

Mia winked at him as his glassy eyes appealed for understanding.

"Then, yak, yak, yak. It's a wonder I don't have another coronary right here from all your talking."

"Promises, promises, old man."

Rolling her eyes, Helen directed her remark at Mia. "You act like a doctor, Mia. The way you're looking at Scout. It's almost like an examination."

Mia purposely ignored her. But she and Jen moved closer. Mia grasped Scout's shoulders and forced him to look her in the eye.

"Go to your doctor. Your pulse is irregular, and you have other symptoms I'm concerned about."

"I'm not going." His shoulders slumped. "I have some medicine at home. I'll take it and rest. I do feel like I'm catching a cold. But no *hospitals*," he said definitely. "I hate those places."

"Please, Scout . . ."

Her pleas fell away as the group slowly made their way through the door of the studio. Helen braced herself under her husband's arm and babbled on.

"Mia, he hates those places. He's going to be okay. I'll make sure he gets what he needs."

She followed them outside and closed the car door on their navy Lincoln Continental. Mia stared at the silver–haired man and his chattering wife as they drove away, leaving her standing alone, unable to help them.

"Adam's got her on the ropes, baby."

J.R. wrapped his arms around Star, and they watched Mia exercise steadily. Her face was a mask of seriousness as she alternated feet and intensity, adding different twists and turns to increase the versatility of each movement.

Unaware of the audience, she moved surely and punched out intermittently, as if she were slaying dragons.

Star hugged him tighter around the waist. "Yeah, kind of like how I've got you, huh?" She pressed her body snugly into his.

They continued to watch Mia through the two-way mirror in the staff lounge at the club for a moment longer, before turning their full attention back to each other.

"Star," he groaned. "Baby, don't touch me like that. I can't stay. I have to go see Adam in a few minutes."

Capturing her hand in his, J.R. stopped the suggestive exploration but rewarded her pouting lips with a soul-stirring kiss.

She pulled away slowly and rose. J.R. watched his lady love
walk to the coffeemaker, and wondered how he could have let
her stay free for so long. She was up to something. She accentu-
ated each swing of her hips with exaggeration, and threw him
a suggestive look over her shoulder. She brought the steaming
mug back to him and sat on the couch.

"Honey?" she purred with a candy-coated voice.

J.R. eyed her suspiciously and leaned back. "No, to whatever
it is you're trying to set me up to do."

"Sweetums," she cooed.

"No, Starlette." He laughed. Falling in love was easy to do
each time he looked into her pretty green eyes. J.R. gave in,
even before he knew what she wanted. "What do you want
me to do? Call the President of the United States and ask him
to lend us the White House for our wedding?"

"Nothing like that," she said, unable to hide the victorious
grin that played along her lips. She put the coffee mug on the
round table and took both his hands.

"I think we should help Adam and Mia."

"Do what?"

"Honey," she said earnestly. "Get *together*. They're such
a cute couple. Don't you think?"

J.R. shook his head as if the notion of cute and them was
totally foreign. "Star, you didn't see them last week in my
office. She looked like she was ready to have his head on a
platter for dinner. And he looked like he could eat her, too."

Star countered with her own argument, reluctant to release
his hands. He wriggled his fingers, trying to extricate them.
"He seemed to be quite interested the other day when we were
over there. He likes her."

J.R. finally shook her free and went back to the two-way
mirror. Mia jabbed three consecutive punches, and he knew he
was about to tread in dangerous waters.

"I don't know, babe," he said reluctantly. "You know how

Adam is about his business. He doesn't like anybody in it. Mia's the same way."

"Honey," Star said as she looped her arm through his, looking at her friend. "She's had it tough this last couple of years. And she needs Adam's love."

She adopted a wistful tone. "Honey, can't you just imagine them together five years from now, with Grace's house full of kids and love?"

"It's meddling, and I don't do that."

"Are you saying you won't help your best friend, the man you love like a brother, your boyhood homie, your ace—"

His lips covered hers with a hunger that ran deep.

When he came up for air minutes later, they both were panting and ready to take their passion home.

Unfortunately, J.R. remembered his plans with Adam.

"Keep my place," he whispered, his lips resting against her mouth.

"Will you help me help them?"

J.R. rested his forehead on hers and wondered when exactly had he fallen in love with her. She probably orchestrated that too, he decided. The pleading in her emerald eyes won.

He swore, giving in. "But if Adam finds out about this, I'm dead."

She squealed her happiness, then gave him a quick peck on the lips. "How about we double at Adam's house this week? Set it up, honey. Don't forget to tell him about the wedding. I love you," she called musically, pushing him into the corridor.

J.R. walked from the room feeling as if a hook, line and sinker had been placed around his neck and he was drowning.

J.R. knew the dirt needed to be turned, then packed around the wood. Adam took the shovel and did it right. They worked the wooden fence in and moved on to the next.

"What's your problem?" Adam asked as they lined the garden on either side with the white wood.

J.R. wiped sweat from his face and took off his work gloves, slapping them against his thigh. They walked back to the screened porch off the back of the house and stepped inside. Adam flipped off the floodlights for the outside and tapped another wall switch to set the ceiling fans in motion.

Cold soda was in the dorm-size ice box he had recently installed in the room. He tossed one to J.R. and popped the top on one for himself. J.R. slumped into the wicker chair, then leaned forward, his hands wrapped around the can.

"I asked Star to marry me, and she said yes."

Adam set the can down. "So answer my question. What's your problem?"

"You mean you aren't mad?"

Adam drew back at this. "Why would I get mad? You and Star are in love, I presume," he said, lifting an expectant eyebrow at him.

J.R. nodded.

"Well, then, it was just a matter of time. I'm happy for you. Congratulations." J.R.'s shocked expression spread into a slow grin that lit up his face.

Adam grinned too. They both looked like silly schoolboys. He shook his best friend's hand. "Come on, let's celebrate."

He hurried to the refrigerator and pulled out some champagne he had gotten from another wholesaler when he won the Striker's Supermarket account a month ago.

Adam searched the cabinets for the crystal flutes and found them enclosed in a custom-made container.

He rinsed the glassed and gathered everything together in his arms, returning to the porch. The bubbly ran over when he poured it. He handed the glass to J.R. and poured one for himself.

"To you and Star. May you have a life full of happiness and love."

They touched glasses and drank. Adam settled on the rattan couch, the sound of crickets pronounced against their silence.

J.R. was too quiet. Adam eyed him closely. The poor guy was probably just worried about getting hitched.

"So why did you think I would have a problem with you and Star getting married?"

"Man, I didn't know what to think. You've been incognito for months. I tried to reach you a couple of times, but you were always busy. I wasn't sure which direction your head was in." J.R. hiccuped, expelling air through his teeth. "I miss Grace, too. Whenever I come here I think of her. Do you think you'll stay here?"

"I've been thinking of selling," he confessed. "This place has a lot of memories. Mom's parties."

They both laughed at the shared memory. "Her and Pops hanging the bathroom wallpaper. You and I hanging out." Adam shook his head, clearing the nostalgia away. "And I started to forget all that, while I was thinking about it being too big for me alone.

"Something just hit me." Adam rubbed the stubble on his chin, his long fingers scratching his head. "This is my place. You and Pops are my family, and selling this house won't make me less—" He didn't want to say lonely. "Alone. So I'm keeping it."

J.R.'s light face broke into a big grin, and he nodded enthusiastically. "I'm glad."

"So, when did you and Star decide to kick things up?"

It was J.R.'s turn to grow serious. "That night after the funeral. I went into the hall closet to get Mrs. Bailey's coat and found Star in there crying. You know how we were. Not making us a priority. Never," he emphasized, "talking about marriage."

Adam shifted and refilled their glasses. He knew how difficult it was for J.R. to change his mind on the subject of matrimony. He used to swear he would never marry. Star must have made all the difference.

"Star helped you through that?"

"No, it wasn't Star. It was Grace."

J.R. began fidgeting with the painting on the wall and moved to the crystal objects that decorated the table. He turned once he got to Grace's rattan rocker, pushing it idly with his hand. Adam got a distinct impression of how his mother had looked sitting in the chair, reading the Sunday paper.

He blinked and it went away.

"Remember the day she asked me to bring her those flannel pajamas in the hospital? Well, she had something in store for me—" J.R. broke off and stared at the floor.

"Anyway, we got into this conversation about love. Adam, she was so alive that day I honestly thought she would beat it. But she basically told me to get serious and marry Star or leave her alone."

The men chuckled. It was just like Grace not to mince words. "'Sometimes adults do things that children don't understand,'" J.R. quoted her, verbatim, "'but in the end, it may not be that you understand, but you accept it and move on'.

"She told me to get on with my life. That I couldn't atone for the mistakes of my parents, but to live the way I wanted to. Right then, I just knew."

He shook his head, an amazed look covering his face.

"I knew I wanted Star as my wife, and the only reason I hadn't done anything about it was because I didn't want to end up hurting my children like my mother did me."

"You're not going to do that," Adam assured him. "You're going to be a great father." This made J.R. grin for a minute. Adam leaned forward. "And I'm going to be a great uncle and godfather to all ten of your children."

They hooted, laughing. "So when's the big day?" Adam asked.

"Six weeks," he said quietly.

"That soon? Any reason?" Adam wiggled his eyebrows.

"No! Star isn't pregnant. She's making me wait, and I don't think I can get past six weeks." Adam sympathized, but didn't want to tell his friend it had been a hell of a lot longer for him.

J.R. grew wistful, nursing his champagne. "Remember when

we used to have the G I Joe Walkie Talkies, and we would hang out of our bedroom windows talking?''

"Yeah, I do." Adam smoothed his hand over his head, leaning back in the chair. His arm caught on the wicker, and he unfastened his watchband, his tan line glowing against his dark skin. "We used to talk so much junk."

"Remember, you wanted three kids. Two boys, and one girl for your wife. You ever think about that now?"

Adam drained his glass. "All the time."

"So what are you gonna do about it?"

The question was a direct hit. Sort of like a torpedo that found its target in a haystack.

"Don't know."

His mood sobered, as earlier thoughts of Candice and her deception returned. It had been unsettling how quiet the day had been. Quite like the calm before the storm.

Adam forced thoughts of tomorrow from his mind. It would get there soon enough.

"So I was thinking . . ." J.R.'s voice lingered in expectation, "that the bride, groom, best man, and maid of honor could get together and discuss wedding plans."

"Man, what are you talking about?"

J.R. slapped his knee and rose. "I said, I thought we would come by and make some decisions about the wedding. We don't have a lot of time."

Adam stood, too. "Sounds like a plan," he said, and slapped J.R. on the shoulder, walking him through the house and onto the driveway.

Adam patted the side of the truck. "Even in the dark, this thing is loud." J.R. faked a punch to his midsection, which Adam pretended to block.

"Yeah, but my baby likes it," he retorted casually, and poked out his chest in masculine one-upmanship.

J.R. got in and Adam backed up to the steps, out of the way of the large wheels. "You sure you don't want to play a couple games of hoops?" J.R. asked hopefully.

"I've got work to do. Next time."

"All right, brother. Star, Mia, and me. Tomorrow, your place." J.R. gunned the engine and shot around the circular drive like lightning.

Mia's coming to my house?

Absently, Adam walked inside, going through the motions of locking up. His thoughts were riveted to different images of Mia. He imagined her in a beautiful wedding gown gliding down the aisle of a church, resplendent and happy. He remembered her mourning in the cemetery. Then laughing when they beat J.R. and Star at cards. Finally, of her last night. "Mmm," he growled.

Her sweet smell lingered. And the way her dark lashes rested on her cheeks when she danced with her eyes closed. He longed to run his fingers through her hair and kiss the pain from her eyes. He wanted them to spark and dance with happiness.

Too much sadness surrounded her, and he wanted to erase it from her eyes. It wasn't easy being the last Webster. But he was lucky. He had J.R., Star, and Pops. And even with them for support, there were times when he still felt like he was alone.

Adam set the house alarm and headed up the stairs, trying to analyze their connection.

She was as unique as the rare roses he searched the world for. She stood alone, separate from every other individual he'd ever met. He would have to find a way to reach out to her. Maybe helping J.R. and Star with their wedding plans would help them get to know one another better.

Adam entered his four room suite. The living room had been transformed into an office, and his laptop sat open, beckoning him. He resisted the urge to sit down, and decided to shower first.

Double French doors opened onto the master bedroom, which was decorated in black lacquer, gold, and hunter green.

He stepped into the black glass shower and tried to imagine

what his life would be like married. He was so ready he could taste it.

Dressed in shorts and T-shirt, Adam sat at the desk and searched his computer for any signs that Candice had begun her vindictive plan. So far everything looked fine, but he could never be sure. He worked late into the night, searching the computer bulletin boards. An item caught his eye, and he downloaded it.

Hotel lobby designs? Tall trees, exotic plants, and fountains. The ideas came faster, and he organized them in a business plan. It was several hours before he switched off the computer. He stripped, heart racing.

Adam crossed his hands behind his head and watched the gold tips of the ceiling fan hit the same spot each tenth of a second. *It has to be practical, yet beautiful,* he thought.

Adam fell asleep dreaming of making it something no one had ever seen before. It had to be awesome. There was a lot at stake.

Chapter 8

"Mr. Webster, something funny is going on. Seventy of Walker's Flower Shops have canceled their orders or refused delivery of their merchandise."

Adam sat in the nine o'clock staff meeting, a pulsing headache fully in charge of his brain. He nodded for the account executive to complete her report. It ended like all the others. The staff stared at him in stupefied silence.

Tentatively, a hand went up in the back.

"Go ahead, Ruth," he said, hoping she had a brilliant idea.

"Sir, are we going out of business?" She tittered. "Because I'm concerned that we won't get paid—"

A low rumbling crawled through the room, and Angela, who sat on his right, looked like she was going to cry.

"Ruth," he called over the increasing grumbles. "None of you have to worry about your jobs." Adam stood, rounding the table to place a supportive hand on her shoulder.

"Everything is going to be fine. Now, the first thing I want you to do is remain calm. We're having a business disagreement with Walker's Flower Shops, though business seems to have very little to do with it." He added the last while rubbing his pounding temples. He sighed.

"I have a call in to Lester Walker," he continued, his voice taking on reassuring tones, "to try to clear up this misunderstanding."

His eyes panned the room, and he was relieved to see that he had reassured at least some of them. Adam grew more confident as he rolled up his sleeves, reclaiming his seat at the head of the table.

"But we have to be prepared. I realize we just received shipments from South America and the Dominican Republic, and we have to do something to move the merchandise or it will die."

"That's correct, sir. The trucks that went out to deliver today's shipments have returned to the warehouse," Teresa, the account executive, added. "But it's full."

Adam resisted the curse that struggled to break free from his mouth. The muscles of his jaw worked as he regained control. Losing it wouldn't help anything.

"Ruth, call the discount distributors. Move as much merchandise as you can, from the oldest inventory first. Start with the merchandise that's not in holding refrigerators. Teresa, call the botanical gardens in all the nearby states. See what they need and supply it.

"Craig, I want you to do this only if we have anything left. Call the downtown hospices and double what we normally give them. And check with Yvonne in new accounts to see if we picked up anything this week. We should have. Tell her she has my permission to cut a deal to get the account and supply it." Everyone hurried out the door, leaving him and Angela alone.

"Angela, tell everyone to be back in here at four o'clock. Also, get me a listing of the second and third level shops who only order periodically from us. Maybe we can offer some deals and move additional merchandise that way."

Adam yanked down his sleeves and put on his suit coat. "I'm going over to Walker's office." The bridled anger in his voice was ready to snap. "If Lester Walker wants a fight, he's going to get one."

Adam stormed past Angela, who lifted her head from her computer then sent the document to the printer. The steady strain of the dot matrix printer interrupted his fury, and he pointed at it, grinding out, "I want that thing out of here today! It's annoying and loud."

He slammed into his office and ripped off his jacket, wishing it was Candice or her father. He paced, alternately jamming his hands in his pockets, then rubbing his head, trying to ease away the headache.

They're trying to ruin me, he thought. Without regard for his hard work or how long it had taken him to build Webster's into the successful company that it was, Lester and his conniving daughter were trying to take it all away.

His calm demeanor hadn't assuaged the angry man, either. It only seemed to infuriate him. Accusing me of killing his grandchildren! Adam shook his head in disbelief and loosened his tie. Candice's cryptic message, delivered through the housekeeper, made his blood run cold.

Size five. Her ring size.

Angela came in just as he threw his jacket into the closet and yanked his tie further away from his throat.

She quietly walked in the mahogany closet and hung up the jacket. By the time she returned, Adam was at the corner window, his hands locked on his hips.

"We have more problems," she started, and Adam sighed. Half turning, he indicated that he was listening.

"The trucking company pulled the trucks and drivers because they can't deliver the merchandise. Right now we have merchandise stacked up at the warehouse, and no way for any of it to get to our other existing accounts. What should we do?"

Adam rolled the sleeves of his pressed white shirt up his arms and prepared for another battle. If Lester wanted to believe

Candice's vicious lie, then so be it, but they wouldn't destroy his life in the process. Candice wouldn't win. His control restored, he said, "Get the trucking supervisor on the phone."

"Yes, sir," she said, and hesitated at the door. "I take it things didn't go well with Lester Walker."

"No, they didn't. But I'm not going to roll over." He was determined. They weren't going to ruin him. He crossed to the desk and sat at the computer and tapped into cyberspace. He would make his way through this situation. He just needed a way in. "Get the supervisor, Angela."

She walked out and buzzed him a moment later.

"Duke's on line one."

Adam picked up the receiver. "Duke, Adam Webster. I understand we have a problem with our trucks and drivers today. I see. Yes. Well, let me make something clear here, Duke. Your guys are under contract to me. Check with the union steward. The drivers can't be called off until three o'clock. It's only one o'clock. I have two hours to get you the new route sheet."

His hardened voice softened when he smiled into the phone. "Of course I can arrange that, Duke. Your mother will love the arrangement I have in mind. I'll make sure personally that it's what you want. No problem. Your wife will get one, too. Great. Thanks, Duke."

Adam sighed in relief and scribbled the last notes before calling Angela.

"Yes, sir?"

"Send a large arrangement to these two addresses. The names are listed. Also, we got the trucks. Tell everybody to hustle. We're on a deadline."

Handing her the paper, he tapped the desk, energized from the exchange and from another item on the Internet bulletin board.

*   *   *

Adam ended the staff meeting late, finally allowing everyone to go home. He expected them back early and knew he wouldn't be disappointed. His staff was loyal and wanted Webster's Wholesalers to survive.

One of the few independent wholesalers in the South, Adam considered himself lucky that he hadn't been sucked up by a chain by now. It had been because of the employees that he hadn't sold out. Many of them had physical handicaps, and hadn't been successful in large corporate environments.

Most worked best alone, and were only too happy to let him be the voice and face representing the company. It was his company, but together they all made it successful.

Adam parked in front of his house and entered through the front door. He threw a steak on the grill, stripping his suit off on his way to the shower. Refreshed within fifteen minutes, he made it to his dinner just in time to save his burning steak.

He sawed into the overdone meat, listening to the kitchen clock tick and the refrigerator hum. When the wind blew, the trees whistled and . . . he was sick of the silence.

He needed company, and hoped only one thing, that after the hellish day he'd had he and Mia would hit it off.

Something needed to go right.

"Star, get over here." Mia pushed the hangers aside. "I can't find anything to wear." Standing in her underwear in the closet, Mia pressed the receiver between her shoulder and ear.

"I'll be right over," Star said, and hung up.

Mia sighed in relief and dropped the phone in the cradle. She sat down on the bed, dejected.

Agreeing to go over to his house?

Mia, you're crazy, she told herself. *You can't attract and reject a man at the same time. He'll think you're a tease.*

She straightened the lace curtain that surrounded the bed and touched the mahogany post with gentle fingers.

Quite an extravagance, she thought, and smiled.

Derrick never would have approved of anything lacy. That could be why she liked it so much. After he got almost everything from their life together, she had allowed herself one bit of pleasure.

Mia slid her hand on the bed, touching the beige comforter. His disapproval had been tough. She had tried to make him happy, but in the end it was impossible.

She was raised to shine. She could be a doctor. Just not a big shot doctor, who made twice as much as he.

Nikki was the last straw. He felt neglected because of the time she spent with their child, and took her birth as a personal insult.

Goose bumps rose on her arms, and Mia searched under a pile of discarded clothes for her robe. He wouldn't have liked that, either. It was short, lavender satin, from Star's favorite place in the mall, Victoria's Secrets.

Mia checked the time and leaned back on the bed, thinking of her life. So much had gone wrong. How had she made such a bad choice? Feelings of inadequacy plagued her, and she went into the bathroom, trying to do something to take her mind off her troubles.

Grabbing a hair bow from the bathroom organizer, she twisted it around her hair and looped it so it hung in a loose knot, halfway down her back.

The phone rang and she hurried to catch it, thankful for the interruption.

"Hello."

"Mia, it's Star. Honey, I can't meet you. Something just came up. J.R. also got another speeding ticket, so I have to pick him up. That red truck excites him too much," she said in good humor.

"That's okay," Mia assured, relieved to have a reason not to go.

"Meet us there."

"We don't have to decide anything tonight. We can do it another time."

"No!" Star broke in fast. "Hold on, Mia. Someone just walked in my office."

Mia listened to the grumbling voices and tried to tamp down her disappointment. She didn't need to see Adam Webster, anyway. Their evening together was a fluke. Nothing at all to get excited about. Yet the disappointment she felt was real.

Star's voice came back through clearly.

"Listen, did you get the last of the directions? You and Adam can spend some time alone."

"No," Mia said adamantly. It was better if they didn't spend any time alone.

"Why?"

"We can do it another time," she insisted, her insecurity growing.

"I think you're scared."

"Of what? Adam?" She hoped her laugh sounded genuine. Despite an extra application of deodorant, she began to sweat. "Star, I'm not scared of anybody," she said, bravado spurning her on. "We're mutual friends of yours. Of course we can sit in the same room and wait for you."

The moment the words were out, her bravado was deflated, and she felt even worse when Star jumped all over them.

"Good, because nothing is going to happen. You don't want a commitment and he doesn't want—whatever."

Papers rustled, and Star whispered to someone.

Mia half listened to the argument and waited for Star to return to their conversation.

"Just meet us there," Star said hurriedly. "You guys can have ten minutes of fun without us, can't you?"

Mia shook off the images of fun Webster style and said, "We'll be fine. Give me the directions."

Mia traced the street address several times on the paper so that it stood out from the rest of the words, and laid it on her bed. She hung up the phone and went back to the closet.

Three outfits were left, and two were automatically disqualified. One dress hung off her like a potato sack. The dark brown color didn't help, either. The other was too tight, and made her look like some of the ladies she'd seen in handcuffs on the news last night, outside the popular strip club in Southeast Atlanta.

The last outfit was a black, one-piece cat suit. It had been her one indulgence when she hit her goal weight over a year ago.

Mia fingered the black, polyester, cotton blend and peeled it off the hanger. The material was soft and flowing as she unzipped the back and stepped into it. It hugged her figure like a second skin. She was awed by her size again as it slid up and encased her.

The material scooped in the front, exposing the rounded curves of her breasts. She sucked in her stomach and looked at herself from the side.

A tiny particle of self-esteem tried to break through and acknowledge that she looked good, but it was trampled by insecurity.

She dragged her jackets forward. *Better cover up,* her common sense warned. She slipped into a masculine cut, double-breasted jacket that hung off her frame.

Mia rolled the sleeves up, grabbed her earrings, and applied makeup to her face. She slid into black ankle boots and finally combed her hair down.

She managed to complete every task without really seeing herself once in the mirror.

Chapter 9

Mia's car coasted to a stop on the circular driveway, and she cut the engine. She promised herself to get a tune-up the following week and stepped out of it, slamming the rickety door.

She stared up at the house, mouth open. It was magnificent. The brick front was elegant and richly designed, and she recognized the signature touch of the house's designer from the landscaping and peaked accents.

Every shrub was perfectly groomed, to the point that they looked like a flat field of greens. Tiny pink, yellow, purple, and red bushes were intermixed with spiked green plants that resembled spiders' legs.

Gathering her courage Mia rang the doorbell, and was surprised when it opened instantly. Adam looked handsome dressed in pressed khaki slacks and a short-sleeved white polo shirt. She drank in the sight of his freshly shaven face, neatly brushed hair, and sexy smile. His feet were bare, she noticed when she looked down. *He's fine,* she admitted.

"Hi," she said, nervously stepping inside and closing the door.

"Hi, yourself."

"J.R. and Star are running late." Mia grinned awkwardly until he took her hand. Raising it to his arm, he looped it through, escorting her in.

"I won't bite, unless you want me to." At her surprised look he said, "I'm joking," but she didn't detect any humor in his voice, or in the expression on his face.

"I knew that," she said, hoping to cover for her sagging knees and pounding heart.

"Come on, I'll show you around. They should be here by the time we finish." They walked through the foyer and onto the screened porch. The minute she stepped outside, Mia fell in love.

"Oh!" she exclaimed at seeing the hundreds of roses that surrounded her. "How much? Where did you? Amazing," she said, touching the delicate blooms. "You did this?" she asked.

"I designed it, and J.R. helped me plant. Over the years I've added on, until now there are over three hundred varieties of roses." He took her hand and followed the red stone that wound through the roses like an intricate maze.

"How much land do you have?"

"Almost three acres. One of which is exclusively garden. The house has a three-car garage, which are those doors over there. The other shed holds tools I use to keep the gardens up. That place way over there is a two bedroom guest house."

"Whose car is that?" she asked, referring to the gold Lexus parked inside the open garage door.

"That was my mother's. Be careful, step over these branches. They have thorns." Mia stepped lightly over the low branches and was taken aback by the majestic beauty of the gardens. There was a multitude of colors, ranging from pale pink, to blue, cream, and coral that edged the walkway.

"These are stunning," she said of the white roses that bordered the sidewalk.

"I planted these along the walkway so that you can see if you're out here and you only have the moonlight to guide you.

These are light enough to help you see your way back to the house.''

They entered an area where the roses looped in figure eight designs and were low to the ground. Mia followed Adam's lead through the colorful carpet of color. She listened intently, asking questions, being careful of the roses that grew in pots. He pointed to them, describing each by name and telling how long it would bloom.

They reached a wooden bridge, and she looked at him questioningly. ''Go ahead,'' he said, following her.

Roses grew high on the wall surrounding a stacked stone enclosure, and she leaned over, thinking it was a well.

''How wonderful,'' she said, delighted when goldfish swam quickly toward the other side of the pond. She sat down facing the pond, and he sat with his back to it, resting his elbows on the stone. ''How many fish are in here?'' she asked, leaning in to stir the water.

''Twenty-four at last count. Did you ever have pets?''

''No. I never did,'' she said, accepting the can of food he got from the stone. ''I wanted to have some for Nikki, though. When she got older. She used to call a dog a bird and a cat a puppy. It was so funny.''

''It sounds like it. I bet you miss her.''

''All the time.'' Birds chirped around them and she looked into the sky.

''Have you ever thought of returning home?''

''You mean to Chicago?''

He nodded.

''No. My folks and I weren't really close, and there really isn't anything there for me. Besides, I like Atlanta. There's a lot of things I want to do and see. I'll probably live here forever.''

''Do you think you'll marry again, maybe have more children?''

''No,'' she said definitely. ''I've had my chance. I've had a husband and a child. The whole kit and caboodle.''

Adam drew his hand up her arm and turned her face to his. She had only to lean over and her head could rest on his shoulder. Or his lips could touch hers. He tilted her face to his.

"What about love, Mia?"

She shook her head and tried to look away. She didn't want him to see the tears that welled in her eyes.

"There's not a whole lot there, Adam. Too much has happened for me to think of love anymore. It's been very disappointing."

"That's not true," he said, tracing the outline of her jaw. "You have the capacity to love and be loved. It's not like food rations, you only get so much and then you've had your quota." He kissed her cheek. "No, it's like one of these flowers." He scooped up a handful of dirt and placed it in her hand.

His eyes met hers. "In your hand is everything you need to make something grow. All the nutrients are there. All we have to do is plant the seed, sprinkle it with a little water, and give it some sun. It will grow, because we're taking care of it. A heart is the same way." His hand closed over hers, and from his powerful fingers she could feel his strength.

"You have to find the right ingredients. Add equal amounts of love and desire. Then sprinkle it with just the right amount of happiness and respect, and it will grow."

He whispered in her ear, "Great sex helps too," at which she laughed. He grew serious again. "I guarantee you that if you get those things, one day you'll look up and recognize that it's right in front of you."

Her eyes locked with his, and Mia desperately wanted to believe him. With him it seemed so possible, so probable, but it was still hard to imagine.

Adam helped her to her feet and they both watched as he peeled her fingers back from the earth in her hand. She brushed it off her hand and he laced her fingers with his.

They walked back along the path to the house.

They finally settled on the sunporch.

"This was my mother's favorite," he said after going into the kitchen for iced tea. He settled next to her on the sofa.

"I can see why. It's so comfortable." She smoothed her hand over the flowered fabric. For a brief second she could imagine a child playing with Legos on the floor. The fantasy evaporated, and she got up and went to the screen-enclosed window.

"Which way does the sun rise?" she asked, gazing out.

Adam tapped her shoulder from behind and pointed in the opposite direction.

It's okay, she told herself when her chest met his in a quick brush as she turned. Mia felt the rush again. It had become synonymous with Adam. Whenever she was with him, she felt that sweet shiver.

His voice was velvet-edged and strong when he spoke against her ear. "Sometimes I would come over and my mother would have all her work spread out on the floor in here. She has," he corrected himself, *"had* a desk right in her room, but she hated the feeling of being closed in."

She turned to him, noting that his voice lacked the sadness she felt whenever she spoke of Nikki. It was reflected in his eyes for a brief moment, though, and she saw it.

"When did you move back?"

"Six months ago," he said, moving around her.

"You gave up your place to take care of your mother?"

He nodded. "I felt I owed her that much, after all the years she took care of me after my father died."

Mia's heart leaped. Her voice lowered to a whisper.

"You obviously loved her very much."

"I loved her the way she loved me. Unconditionally."

"That's wonderful—"

"You deserve it, too—"

They both spoke at the same time, oblivious to the other's last words. Adam plunged his fingers through her hair, and she arched toward him.

His lips against hers felt foreign and different. She didn't know what to do, so she let go and opened for him. The second she felt the probe of his tongue her eyes drifted closed, letting her mouth slowly accept the sweet pleasure he was giving to her.

He brought her closer and he continued the leisurely exploration of her mouth. And she liked it. Every second of it.

Just friends, echoed in her head and she stepped away, covering her mouth with her hand. Her moisture stayed on his mouth and he didn't bother to rub it off, like she did. Adam drew his lower lip in and sucked it off before releasing it.

Mia wanted to die.

"The bathroom," her normally husky voice croaked. "I need to use the bathroom."

"Down the hall, on the right."

Mia leaned back against the door, panting. She ran a towel under the sink and patted her flushed face. Looking in the mirror, she cringed. God, she looked wanton.

Where in the world were Star and J.R.? This wasn't supposed to be happening. Everyone was supposed to be together. Her thoughts ran back to the conversation she had with Star. Had that been J.R. in the background?

She didn't have time to think anymore, because she realized she had been in there for about ten minutes. Mia heard the phone ring. They must be on their way. *Thank you.*

Adam had his back to her when she entered the kitchen. He cradled the phone on his shoulder and held a steaming pot with both hands. The conversation was about business, but she could tell he was talking to a woman.

He kept calling her "Ange." She assumed it was short for Angela. A bubble of jealousy burst in her stomach, and she backed away from the door.

Adam spotted her, and she signaled that she was leaving. He put the pot down, shaking his head.

"Hold on," he said to the caller. His confused gaze pinned her in place. "Where are you going?"

"I'll just leave. I see that you're busy," she said, letting her words drift. Mia turned, walking toward the door.

"This is my secretary," he said from behind her. "It will only take another minute. I popped us some popcorn. We can catch a movie until J.R. and Star get here."

Adam sighed heavily and put the pot on the unlit burner before picking up the phone and holding it against his chest. "Stay, okay? I've had a hell of a day and I could really use some friendly company."

Into the phone he said, "Goodbye, Angela," and hung up the wall unit.

Mia tried to walk away, but she couldn't leave him with his bowl of popcorn, bottle of wine, bare feet and tired expression. She didn't know what changed her mind. She couldn't say it was the strain in his voice when he talked on the phone, or his bare feet.

She identified with the look in his eyes when he said he'd had a long day and wanted some companionship. How many times had she wished Derrick would understand when she uttered those very words, so long ago?

A kindred spirit rose within her, and she peeled off her jacket. "Okay, I'll stay."

"Very nice." He whistled appreciatively.

She tipped her head and sighed. "Oh, I forgot," Adam said. "You're the only woman I know who doesn't want anyone to tell her she's beautiful." He led the way to the den and put the refreshments on the table.

"Should I start calling you mug muffin?" he asked, sitting down, stretching his long arms across the back of the couch.

She burst out laughing, despite herself, sitting beside him. "You'd better not."

Mia couldn't remember a time when she'd had more fun. They argued politics, disagreed about sports, discussed favorite foods and finally found they shared something in common. They both liked the old Lakers basketball team.

"I love them," Mia said before filling her mouth full of hot buttered popcorn.

"You love them?" he scoffed, teasing. "Now see, that's the difference between men and women. We *like* basketball. Women *love* everything."

She pretended to poke him. "Just for that, I won't tell you which championship game I recently went to, and who's autograph I got."

Adam's eyes widened. "Who?"

"I'm not telling," she said, then yelped in surprise.

Adam had snatched her feet onto his lap and was unlacing her boots. "Did you know feet are a great place to torture someone when they have information you want?"

She didn't believe he would do it until he ripped her sock from her foot. "You wouldn't," she said incredulously.

"You pushed me too far. Tell," he demanded.

She squeezed her lips closed and he started tickling. Mia kicked, giggling until she couldn't take it anymore. "Okay. Philadelphia."

He stopped instantly. "Philadelphia? That wasn't recently. That had to be at least twenty years ago."

They both burst out laughing. "Whose autograph did you get?"

"The Doctor's, of course," she said, straightening her outfit.

"I can't believe you had me going like that," Adam said after he popped the movie into the VCR.

Mia felt comfortable now, sitting next to him. His long legs stretched forward and the heels of his feet dug into the thick pile of carpet. It felt soft under her feet. She was glad her feet were bare, too.

The sunken den was huge, with a black leather sectional sofa that sat before a large-screen television. Three other separate armchairs filled the room, along with blown glass tables, and accenting lamps.

Adam pushed the remote and leaned forward, taking a handful of popcorn. He tossed each one in the air, catching it in his mouth.

Her thigh tingled when his leg rubbed against it, but he kept it there, and she didn't move, either.

"I'm going to be out of the country for a couple of weeks. I leave next Saturday."

"Really? Why?" Her heart doubled its beat, and her hands grew clammy. Mia wanted to believe the riptide of emotions wasn't because of the possibility of not seeing Adam for a while.

"I've got to make new contacts for my business. I let one component in my business become too large, and now that they're looking to take their business elsewhere I've got to look at other opportunities."

"Like what?" she questioned, wanting to delve deeper into his too patent answer. Both ignored the first action scene of the movie.

"I have a couple of ideas." He grabbed a cloth napkin and wiped his mouth. "One especially feels good. I'm going to go with that first."

"What will you do if it doesn't work out?"

He shrugged. "Find something else. There's lots of opportunities out there. I just have to find the right one."

His positive response belied his serious expression.

"That sounds interesting," she said, noticing how tense he was. She wasn't surprised when he took her hand, urging her close to him. Adam stared at the television for a while, and she dragged her eyes from their locked fingers.

"Is your business in trouble?"

His shoulders squared, and he raised his head.

"Nothing I can't handle," he said confidently, and she believed him.

"You seem so passionate about your work. I once felt the same way about medicine."

He patted her knee and took her hand again. "It's easy to

love what I do. I enjoy making people happy. I suppose you could say the same thing about healing.''

''I guess so,'' she said, flicking at lint on her leg. ''It doesn't always work, no matter how hard you try and no matter what you do.''

''But that's part of the process, Mia. Sometimes you can't save them all.''

''No, not all the time,'' she said. Mia slid down deeper in the sofa, to get comfortable. She tried to keep her head from gravitating toward his shoulder as she watched the action adventure film, but couldn't resist. Adam never acknowledged that she laid her head there and neither did she. He just scooted down, giving her complete access to his shoulder.

Just two friends watching a movie, having a good time, she reminded herself.

Chapter 10

Three peals of the antique grandfather clock roused Mia slowly from the erotic dream. The realistic visions held her eyes closed as she tried to stop the passion from fading. She snuggled closer and was rewarded with a masculine sigh of contentment and the warmth on her back by strong arms.

Coming fully awake, she kept her eyes closed and held her breath, realizing the arrhythmic breathing was not her own. Cracking one eye open, Mia spotted a broad white polo shirt that was pulled tight across an impressive chest. *Adam's.* A late night movie was on the television, the adventure movie long finished.

Adam lay sleeping by her side, his arms holding her close to his chest. What surprised her more was the way her leg draped over his, pinning him in. And her hand!

She wasn't even thinking about the one pressed against his chest. She was more concerned about the one that was snugly smashed between his thighs.

She grew hotter, considering if he moved even an inch, her hand would be full. She coughed, not wanting to consider the possibilities.

Adam breathed deeply and shifted, and Mia pulled her hand

free. She moved her leg, also, but so did he. He wedged his thigh between her parted legs. The shift might as well have been on the earthquake fault line, because that's how electric the heat was, between Adam and the black leather.

Mia lay still for a few moments, gathering her wits. His skin was so smooth that she raised her hand, then dismissed the idea of touching him. But the seed had already been planted.

Lowering her hand, she caressed the sinewy muscles of his arms, over his rounded elbow to his brawny hands.

His chest was broad, and she let the tips of her fingers skim over the rippled muscles.

Good grief. He felt good.

Mia glanced into his face to make sure he was still asleep before she continued. She grew bolder, as did her excitement, until she panted aloud when her hand passed over the rounded side of his hip leading to his taut bottom.

She froze when gunfire erupted on the television, bursting the silence in the room.

Her eyes slapped closed and she wanted to turn to dust and blow away.

Adam stirred, and she prayed that he would fall back asleep so she could quietly get up and go home.

Discovery time was over.

But he didn't fall back asleep. The nap seemed to energize him.

Their breath intermingled, and she still kept her eyes closed, and she dared her heart to cease the locomotive rhythm. No such luck. When his lips moved closer, she had only to purse and they would meet.

She didn't have to. Because he did.

Mia let him kiss her, hoping it would end, praying it would last forever. It felt that good.

When her lips parted for his searching tongue she knew she was heading for troubled waters, but was unable to stop the slide.

Adam rolled her beneath him, pressing her deep into the

sofa, searching the hidden treasures of her mouth, and Mia relaxed her lips, accepting with delight the joy he was giving.

He groaned and ground into her lightly, sending currents of pleasure from her center outward. His kisses took on a new life as they slid down her lips to her neck. Adam seemed intent on finding her most sensitive spot, where she had to respond, had to acknowledge that he was giving her pleasure.

Mia gripped the couch, alternating between gasps and sighs of abandon. Whenever she took a breath he moved lower, and she arched her back, wanting to give him what he sought.

The stretchy material of the cat suit moved down each inch he moved until the rounded tops of her breasts were exposed. He gently kissed the curve, then sucked it, and she gritted her teeth, wanting to cry out. Wanting more.

''You're beautiful,'' he moaned, his arm lifting her while he eased the back zipper down several inches.

Her desire shifted into overdrive when he slipped his hand into the lace and freed her breast. *Touch it,* her body demanded through a thick haze of desire.

Adam did one better, making each toe curl and her leg jump. He covered it with his tongue and licked up, then down, until her ragged breathing got so loud it bounced off the walls.

Her fingers dug further into the sofa and she fought the undulating motion of her hips, unable to resist his grinding.

Sweetly, he tortured her when he covered her peaked flesh with his mouth and sucked her in.

Mia moaned her appreciation, her hands latching onto his back, touching his hot skin.

''Mia, I want you,'' Adam rasped, molding the pimpled tip of her breast between his thumb and forefinger. He pressed into her center, making his point. She responded back.

Then she froze.

The heated excitement she'd been feeling turned to naked fear. Mia lay paralyzed beneath him. She shook her head mutely.

Adam misunderstood her silent answer.

"I have protection," he murmured, grasping handfuls of her hair, kissing her forehead.

"No," she cried out, adding more strength to her voice. She must be crazy to be in this position. Besides, sex had hidden meanings like commitment, marriage, and children—all of which she'd once had and lost. There was no way she would travel a road filled with pain-filled potholes again.

"No, I've got to go. I'm sorry," she cried, thrusting with her body to indicate she wanted to get up.

"What is this?" Adam demanded.

It was magnificent! And alarming, she wanted to scream as she scrambled off the sofa, searching the floor for her purse. The small bag was draped over the edge of the couch, the long corded strap blending into the smooth leather. The television station ended viewing for the evening and signaled with a long peal.

It was the end for her, too. She grabbed her shoes, more determined than ever to leave.

"I don't understand," Adam said as she rushed around looking for her coat. The cat suit was suddenly very ridiculous, and she was sorry she wore it. Mia fumbled, trying to fix her bra and zipper at the same time, giving up on finding her jacket.

She had no business being there, she told herself as she hurried to the front door.

"Mia?" Adam questioned, quietly. "What just happened here?" She reached for the doorknob, and he touched her hand. Hot tears gathered in her eyes. She fought them, unwilling to cry.

"I made a mistake coming over here. Forget this evening ever happened."

"I can't," he said plaintively. "I won't ever forget. Neither will you."

"Yes." She nodded, her anguish at what she had been about to do surrounding her like a thick fog. "I'm not the fun person you want me to be. I'm not a good time girl. I have to be alone."

Looking into his eyes proved fatal, and she wished she hadn't. They raked her, full of concern, searching for answers she wouldn't give.

Mia hurried outside and had almost made it to the car when his hand on her arm stopped her flight.

"I want to talk to you," he said cooly, the tone of his voice making her stop. "Something is happening between us. I want to talk about it."

"I didn't mean for this to happen. I thought I could just be friends with you, but I can't. Adam, I'm not somebody you want to get to know. I don't want anyone to know me. Do you understand?"

"Is that why you left medicine?" he probed, ignoring what she'd said. "Because everyone who knows you is there?

"You're mysterious, and intriguing and smart. You know how I know? Because the few times we've had a conversation when your guard wasn't up were pleasant and enjoyable."

Mia steadily shook her head, her curls bouncing. "I left medicine because you're always *On*. You can't forget, you can't miss an opportunity, you can't freeze, or someone will die." She yanked on the handle of the car and the rusted door protested.

"Who died?" he asked, catching her by surprise.

The one person I couldn't save. "Nobody," she moaned, inserting the key in the ignition. The car dragged and didn't start. She pumped furiously and tried again. It dragged slower, then stopped.

"Tell me what happened," he said, his hand on the door.

"I don't want to talk about it," she said, trying to still her trembles. Mia turned the key again, and got no response. She gritted her teeth and banged the steering wheel with her hand. If he kept asking, she would fill him so full of her life he wouldn't be able to handle it. She wouldn't burden anyone with the troubles of her past.

Especially not him.

He blew out in exasperation. "You don't want to talk about

it?'' His usually easygoing temperament gave way to frustration and anger.

"Well, I do. Let me tell you something. I've probably had the worst day of my career, and I want to forget about it.

"Today, somebody that used to be in my life told a lie that might destroy the business I've struggled to build for eleven years. I have twenty-three employees who depend on me for their bread, and I may have to lay them off if this person has their way, because what they're asking is not something I want to give. Tonight all I wanted was to be with my friends, but when you showed up at my door it was as if my prayers were answered. I don't know about you, but I get tired of being alone." His anger lessened, and he lowered his voice. She listened, staring out the windshield, unable to look at him.

"Tonight might have been too soon, but it wasn't a mistake." When she didn't respond he reached inside the car and took the keys out of the ignition and pocketed them.

"Just what do you think you're doing?" she asked, suspicion lacing her voice.

"I'm going to give you a ride home. Let me get my shoes."

Mia covered her face as soon as he disappeared into the house. She wanted to cry so much that her tear ducts ached.

She was ashamed of her behavior, and the fact that she had read him so wrong. He had his own personal problems, yet he was still concerned with her feelings.

Gathering herself, she locked and closed the car door, wishing she could click her heels and disappear. Adam returned with her forgotten jacket, and she slipped it on, careful to avoid touching him.

The ride seemed interminable. She sat stonily, relieved when the domed lights of her apartment complex loomed ahead.

Adam stopped the car, cutting the engine and headlights. "Mia," he began, but stopped when she raised her hand and opened the door. The car bells rang.

Her eyes ached for release, and she resisted the urge to run. Bathed in faded gold light, he looked tired and confused, and she hurt that she couldn't tell him what lay on her heart. It was better this way, she reasoned.

"Adam, I can't be your friend, or anything else, for that matter. I never want to see you again."

Chapter 11

"Is it business or pleasure that has you all tied up in a knot?"

Adam looked into Star's sympathetic face and almost confided in her, then changed his mind. He didn't need his friends to bail him out of his problems.

"I appreciate your concern, but I have everything under control. Nothing is going on that I can't handle."

"Is it Mia?"

Just the mention of her name conjured up memories so strong that he grew physically uncomfortable trying to control himself.

"Have you spoken to her?" he asked.

"No, I haven't. Should I?"

Noncommittally, he shrugged his shoulders. "I don't know, Star. Do whatever you want. I don't mean to sound rude, but did you want something specific?"

"I thought we could go to lunch. I wanted to tell you about my new promotion."

"That's great, hon," he said absently. "What exactly do you do? You always say something like, 'a little of this and a little of that'."

She laughed. "I still do the same thing, a little of this and that, only I have a title. Executive Director of Interpersonal Relations.''

Adam looked at her blankly.

''I'm a government liason. When we have difficulty with a foreign diplomat or his family or children, or something of that nature, something delicate, I handle it.'' She waved evasively.

''That's big time,'' Adam said, admiring her. ''Lots of classified stuff, huh?''

''Afraid so,'' she said, and grabbed her bag. ''I still need to talk flowers with you for the wedding. But it can wait.''

Pushing to his feet, Adam rounded the small table and hugged her. ''I hope I didn't hurt your feelings earlier. I just have a lot on my mind.''

''I bend, but I don't break.''

The discreet beep of the intercom buzzer halted any further discussion. Angela's voice cut into the silence.

''Adam, sixteen more of Walker's stores have canceled their orders.''

During all the years they had worked together, Adam had never heard her sound worried.

''There's more,'' she said, grimly.

Adam pressed the button and picked up the phone.

''Angela, first assemble the team and get them in here. When everyone is present, we'll begin.''

He turned back to Star. ''I'm sorry. Can you hold on a minute? I've got to handle something.''

The group gathered quickly in his office, all eyes weary with concern. ''Yvonne, any new accounts?''

''Yes, sir,'' she said, enthusiastically. Applause split the room, along with sighs of relief.

''Who is it?''

''The specialty store Thunder is going to pilot a floral shop in two of its stores. If it works, then they'll expand to ten by the end of the year, and the remaining fifty by the end of next year.''

''So we've only in actuality picked up two?'' The enthusiasm

WE HAVE 3 FREE BOOKS FOR YOU!

(If the certificate is missing below, write to:
Zebra Home Subscription Service, Inc.,
120 Brighton Road, P.O. Box 5214, Clifton, New Jersey 07015-5214)

FREE BOOK CERTIFICATE

Yes! Please send me 3 *Arabesque* Contemporary Romances without cost or obligation, billing me just $1 to help cover postage and handling. I understand that each month, I will be able to preview 3 brand-new *Arabesque* Contemporary Romances FREE for 10 days. Then, if I decide to keep them, I will pay the money-saving preferred subscriber's price of just $12.00 for all 3...that's a savings of almost $3 off the publisher's price with no additional charge for shipping and handling. I may return any shipment within 10 days and owe nothing, and I may cancel this subscription at any time. My 3 FREE books will be mine to keep in any case.

Name _____

Address _____ Apt. _____

City _____ State _____ Zip _____

Telephone ( ) _____

Signature _____ AR0996
(If under 18, parent or guardian must sign.)

in the room dampened. He hated to make it sound so cut and dried, but that was the reality.

"How soon? Do they have the equipment?"

"Yes sir, it should be there next week."

"Call them. Offer our crew to help with the setup. We don't want the plants to die and then have them blame us, saying our merchandise is bad. Any others?" He turned to Teresa.

"We're in a holding pattern. Nobody is increasing their orders, even though we've offered awesome discounts."

Star slipped out of Adam's office unnoticed and sat at a corner desk. Picking up the phone, she dialed quickly.

"Jamal, Starlette Baxter. Yes, I need something checked out for me. Yes, the works."

What she hadn't told Adam was that she not only handled interpersonal relations, but she also knew people in banking, hotels, and airlines, among others.

Sometimes, she had to act fast and needed the help of others.

Jamal Craer was one of her street contacts. He was the best private investigator in the south, and a good man to have on your side.

Jamal's voice snapped her back from the spinning thoughts. "Do the works on Walker, Lester. As in flower shops. I want to know everything. How soon? Yesterday."

The insistent tapping began again as Mia lay staring blankly at the door. Ignoring the knock, she covered her head, unsuccessfully trying to block out Star's voice.

Relenting, she dropped her feet to the floor, dragging them over to the door. Pressing her ear against it, she listened, hoping Star would give up and go away. Star slapped the door, and she jumped.

"Mia, open the door! I mean it. Your steps are covered with—stuff. I know you're in there. Open up!"

Mia snatched the door open and Star stumbled inside.

"What is it?" Mia braced her hands firmly on her hips. Star moved first, and gave Mia a big, warm hug.

"I should be pissed at you, but you look like you needed that."

Star stepped aside and pointed. "Take a look at what an admirer left you."

Mia peeked out, and on each of the sixteen steps leading to her door were two crystal vases, each holding twelve beautiful roses, in every shade, shape and size. Her stairs looked like a beautiful garden pathway.

"Oh no, he didn't," Mia moaned behind her hand.

"I bet he's sorry for whatever he did," Star joked softly. "Don't you think we should bring them in, so when the delivery man comes back with more he'll have someplace to put them?"

"I never even thought of that. Wait a sec, I've got to change." She hurried to the closet and yanked out some sweatpants.

"We're only going to the steps." Star stared at her. "Your cutoffs are fine."

"Please Star, don't work me too close. Today is a bad day."

Star quirked her lips. "You're not as square as I thought."

They formed a two person assembly line, passing vases to each other until all the flowers were inside. The small apartment grew more confined, overwhelmed by the large, aromatic bouquets. Each vase contained a card. Mia gathered them together unread and placed them in the night table drawer, closing it with a resounding thud.

"Don't you want to see what he has to say?" Star asked, unable to resist a look at the drawer. She stared at Mia expectantly.

"No, I don't. Adam and I aren't friends. In fact, none of this was even necessary." She made a sweeping gesture with her hand, encompassing the room. Mia lifted a vase of bright red roses and sat on the couch, lowering it to the floor beside her feet. She hoped to avoid any discussion of her and Adam.

"So what brings you to my neck of the woods on such a beautiful day? Aren't you supposed to be at work?"

"I came by to check on my good friend who hasn't been to work since Sunday, and who hasn't answered her phone or her door in three days. I was worried about you."

Mia smiled and patted her friend's hand. "You don't need to worry about me. I'm fine." Mia shifted uncomfortably. "Don't look at me with those cat eyes." She laughed shortly. "You make it impossible for me to talk."

"Mia, I'm your friend. We can talk about anything. It's obvious something is bothering you. First of all, this place is spotless. Even the baseboards. That's the first sign of a woman with something on her mind.

"Second, you have the same hollow look as Adam. You both look like you lost your best friend."

"When did you see him?" Mia hated herself for asking, but she had to know. She leaned forward, waiting for the answer.

"Earlier this week. I went to his office to ask for his help with the flowers for the wedding, but he was swamped with work. He's having a tough time. He looked absolutely bone weary."

Mia felt worse. She hadn't tried to hear what he had to say on those days when he had come knocking on her door.

Now, the flowers. The evening hadn't even been his fault. Mia tugged her ear.

"I guess you won't believe that I just wanted to take a couple of days off." She shrugged at Star's disbelieving look. "I didn't think so."

She gathered her courage, closing her eyes, blocking out the flowers. "I tried to seduce Adam," she said flatly. "And when it didn't work, I told him I never wanted to see him again."

Rising, she moved around the vases and sat on the bed. She held up her hand. "There's more. I ran out of his house half dressed, and then my car wouldn't start, so he had to give me a ride home."

"Girl, you're lying!" Star's mouth hung open. "I can't believe it. *You?* Well I guess I can understand you trying to get some, but what I can't imagine is him turning you down! Did he say why not?"

"Star," she warned.

"Girl, in for a penny, in for a pound. Come on, tell me," Star urged, leaning closer.

Exhaling a deep breath, Mia whispered the confession.

"It wasn't him. He wanted to—" She gestured with her hands. "Go on. I stopped things."

"You what!"

Mia nodded and Star stared.

"Mia, that can't be all. Let me get this straight. You started this seduction thing. He said yes, and you were saying yes, then you said no. Am I right so far?"

Mia nodded.

"What happened? Didn't you want to anymore?"

"What I *want* is beside the point. I can't see him again, Star. He probably thinks I'm some sex starved maniac who's emotionally unstable. I'm embarrassed at what I did."

"Uh-huh." Star nodded, dragging the words. "How long has it been?"

Mia responded quietly. "Almost three years."

"Quit lying!" Star gasped. "Well, no wonder! I probably would have jumped him, too! And I promise you, I would have finished—" Mia winced.

"Sorry." Star dragged a pink rose from the vase and sniffed. "Mia, it's natural. You've been celibate for a long time. It's perfectly natural for your body to have needs and a desire for them to be met. Especially by someone as special as Adam."

"But Star, I've told him so often that I don't want to date anyone. Then I go to his house, and show out. I can't believe myself." She blushed, embarrassed. "So now you know why I've been hiding. I thought I should take a couple of days off to get myself together."

"Don't you think he would understand if you explained it to him?"

Mia shook her head. "You didn't see his face when we were

outside his house. He feels sorry for me. I know he doesn't need a pathetic woman in his life. He even tried to tell me how bad a day he had, and I didn't try to listen. I'm not like that normally. I wanted to, but I didn't.''

She swallowed the lump in her throat. "He seems like a wonderful person, and he deserves someone that can be his emotional equal. Lately I've been a basket case."

"You're doing well. You've just dealt with the death of your child. Nobody is expecting you to be Superwoman."

"I've never made a pass at anyone before. Not even my ex-husband. But Adam is different. I wanted to. Then I froze."

"So what are you going to do now?" Star asked. "Wait three more years until another Prince Charming comes along and sweeps you off your feet? Girl, you might not get that lucky." She laughed, her green eyes dancing. "So, what's a little egg on your face? I've heard it builds character."

Mia rolled her eyes, a small smile curving her lips.

The phone interrupted them and Mia let the machine pick it up.

The voice at the other end surprised her.

"Doctor Jacobs, this is Theresa Humboldt from Doctor Charles Hawkin's office. We've been trying to reach you for some time, but since we haven't been able to catch up with you, could you call Doctor Hawkins at three-one-two."

Snatching up the receiver, Mia turned her back on Star.

"Theresa, Doctor Jacobs here. Yes, I'm fine. Is Doctor Hawkins okay? Oh, good. Well then, what can I do for him? He'll be here when?" She scribbled on a notepad. "Yes, of course. Tell him I would be delighted to meet with him. Just tell him to call me when he gets here. Good to hear from you, too. Take care. Bye."

Mia answered a knock on the door before Star could start in on her. "Ms. Jacobs?"

"What is this?" Shocked at the size of the package, Mia automatically stepped back. Clear cellophane paper and a huge pink bow prevented her making out what was inside.

"It's a twenty pound chocolate bunny. It was special made at the chocolate factory. See you in two hours."

"What? Why?" she asked, struggling to get the bunny on the already full counter.

"We have orders to bring a dozen roses every two hours."

"No. Don't deliver any more." Mia lessened the sharpness in her tone. "I'm sorry." She read his name tag. "Cliff. I'll put a stop to this right now. Have a good night," she said before closing the door behind him. Star opened her mouth to say something, and Mia sent her a dark look, then picked up the phone. She opened the drawer and read the envelope of one of the cards Adam had sent and dialed the number.

"This is Mia Jacobs. Please cancel any future deliveries to this address. I won't accept any more. Thank you."

She hesitated, then slowly peeled up the flap of the envelope. Mia closed her eyes, pressing it to her breast, the words emblazoned on her lids for her personal viewing.

"When we make love, the time will be right for us both. I'm willing to wait. Love, Adam." Involuntary shivers coursed through her, shaking her, making her remember.

"Who's Doctor Hawkins?" Star cut in. "A new flame?"

Chapter 12

Star rushed up the stairs ahead of Mia, rain pelting them in big drops. The rug around the door was dark from the puddles their shoes made when they entered. Shrugging off her coat, Mia gave it to Star, who hung it over the tub with hers.

Mia peeled open a container of steamed rice and spooned some into the center of the plate.

"Charles Hawkins is not a mystery man. He's a colleague from Chicago who I haven't seen in a while."

Star peered at her closely. "You're not interested in him?"

"No."

"He's not interested in you?"

"No," Mia insisted.

"If you say so," Star replied, and opened her Szechwan shrimp. She stole a piece of Mia's pepper steak while talking. "Finish telling me about Derrick. Didn't you know he didn't want kids before you got married?"

"He always said maybe. I always held out hope that it was just fear that made him hesitate." Her eyes clouded.

"There was a big hepatitis scare, and I spent several days and nights at the hospital and didn't take the pill. It just so happened that on that rare occasion we made love, and I got pregnant."

"He obviously didn't take it well."

Mia stopped pushing her food around her plate. "He got very angry, then silent. He started drinking more heavily. Then he got suspended for showing up in court intoxicated." Mia stared into the distance, unseeing.

"It all snowballed for us. I tried to help him. But he saw it as my fault. Like I trapped him. I didn't."

"I know," Star offered sympathetically. "That must have hurt you financially," she said, biting into her shrimp.

"It didn't. We were making a six figure salary. I had been written up in medical journals, and was very popular with my colleagues, who referred additional work to me." Her voice flattened.

"Derrick hated it. He vowed he would never lift a hand to help me with the baby. He said I was just trying to overshadow his career with my own. I realized then, I had made a big mistake."

Mia lifted the picture of her and Nikki from the shelf and smiled sadly.

The little girl's smile mirrored hers, only she had eight teeth. Four at the top and four at the bottom. Her pug nose was turned up, and Mia recalled how hard she tried to make Nikki's bang lay down. The hair wouldn't cooperate, so in the picture it stood straight up on her head.

Derrick had disappeared into the scenery of her life after Nikki. Not because she wanted him to, but because he chose to be there.

"He wouldn't seek help for the alcoholism, and it just got worse. Then Nikki drowned." Mia stopped abruptly, swallowing the emotion. "Nothing could ever be proven, but it was suspected that he may have been drunk when she fell in the pool and drowned."

Horror touched Star's face and Mia hated that she had lain

her whole life on the table for her friend. Star looked wistfully at the picture, then placed it on the shelf.

"I'm so sorry. I had no idea."

"It's not something I tell people every day. I loved her so much it still hurts today. She was such a lovable child. When Doctor Hawkins handed her to me, I thought she was smiling."

"Is that the same man whose secretary called?"

Mia nodded.

"What do you suppose he wanted?"

"Me back," she said and looked at her friend. "He planned to start a private practice. I suppose he's calling to offer me a chance to join him."

Mia took her plate to the sink, then sat on the floor, crossing her legs. The table lamp cast a golden, calming glow. She reached for a rose in the vase next to her and tugged it out.

Star sat on the floor, too. "Do you want to go back?"

Mia sighed. It wasn't that easy to decide. She glanced at the cluttered floor, reminded of the complications in her life. She couldn't answer.

"Don't you miss it?"

Mia nodded. "Of course I do. I loved working with the children. My greatest joy was being able to make a difference in a child's life. Sometimes I'm almost to the phone, ready to call Scottish Rite or Charles Hawkins and tell him I'm on my way. Then I remember . . . Nikki. I couldn't save her." She finally broke down.

"I got home too late," she sniffled, her voice thick with tears. "My secretary told me the school called, and when they couldn't get hold of me they called Derrick. I couldn't believe he picked her up, but then I got scared. Very scared. He was constantly drinking, and I knew he had started early that morning. I raced home, but . . ." Her voice dropped off. Tears streaked in a path down her face, and she fought for control.

"I was too late. I tried to revive her, but I couldn't. I couldn't do anything to bring her back."

"Where was he?"

"He wasn't there when I got there. He claims he heard me come in and took off with friends, but I never believed that. I couldn't take the pain of seeing sick children anymore, so I quit."

"You can't hide forever. Think of it another way. There would be lots more sick children if it weren't for people like you who dedicate their lives to helping others.

"Mia, you hold miracles in your hands. You've been blessed. Don't bury your godgiven talent with your child.

"Now, as for Adam. You and I both know he's not the bad guy here."

Mia sniffled and accepted the tissue that Star handed to her. She pushed her hair behind her ear, then sniffed the rose. It was one of the ones she'd admired from his garden. Adam was trying to blackmail her. She'd told him it was one of her favorites.

"I knew you would get back to him eventually." Mia hesitated, then sheepishly confessed, "I get this rush every time I'm near him." She shyly glanced away. "It's very sexual."

Star clapped and did a victory cheer. She kicked up her short legs and knocked over one of the vases. Both grabbed for it at the same time, laughing.

"Go with it," she advised. "It's been so long, you need to have some fun. Don't be afraid."

Mia rose and parted the curtain at the window, watching the rain streak the glass.

Star came to stand beside her. "How does it feel when he touches you? Do you feel like you're on fire? Like you can't wait for the pleasure to end? Yet you want it to stay forever?" Star touched her arm and Mia turned.

"Whether you know it or not, you're on the way back. All I'm asking is for you to try to imagine a future without him." Everyone seemed to know more about her situation than her.

"I've got to go. Can J.R. expect you at work tomorrow?"

"Yes." Mia slapped her forehead. "Can I get a ride to work? The last time I saw my car it was dead on Adam's driveway."

"Sure. I can take you."

"Star." Mia shot her a warning glance. "It'd better be you in the morning. Not him. I noticed how you and J.R. never showed up the other night."

Star shrugged, her face the picture of innocence. "We were busy. We're not trying to matchmake."

"Who said anything about matchmaking, you little sneak?"

Star ran to the bathroom, laughing and dancing around the dozens of roses that crowded the floor. She looked as bright as a fire engine when she came out, with her red shiny raincoat, auburn hair and cheery disposition. Mia couldn't stay mad at her.

"No funny tricks. Oh, by the way, I took the liberty of choosing an absolutely adorable dress for you for the wedding."

"You what?"

"After all," Star cut her off, a sly look crossing her face, "my maid of honor must be absolutely smashing."

"I would love to be in your wedding." Mia smiled for the first time that night.

"Well, good. I'd better go. J.R. will be wondering where I am. I wonder what Adam is doing tonight. He's probably lonely and confused, the poor darling."

"Goodnight, Star," Mia said, closing the door on her happy giggle.

Chapter 13

Adam slumped into the chair in J.R.'s office and waited. His week had been grueling. The loss of business from Walker's was impacting overhead so heavily that personnel decisions would have to be made about layoffs if something didn't come up.

As it was, he was scrambling every day to distribute inventory, and other shops had heard of his troubles with Walker's. They were demanding outrageous discounts or threatening to take their business elsewhere.

This was the only place he could relax, yet his troubles followed him. Candice was trying to bury him. So far, her shovel was full of dirt.

A knock at the door forced him from his personal thoughts. "J.R., the headphones in the studio are broken again . . ." Adam was shocked to see Mia's head pop in the door. Her long black hair was braided, and she had woven gold threads through it to match the gold in her workout clothes. She was absolutely, without question, the most beautiful woman in the world.

"Mia we have to talk," he said when she turned and started to walk away. She slipped into the ladies' locker room before he could catch up with her, and he waited outside until the door opened.

"Tell Mia I'm not leaving until we talk."

"Mia isn't in there," Ester said, looking at him strangely. "She left through the emergency door."

He bristled and stalked into the aerobics studio. J.R. was working behind the sound system. Adam knocked on the cabinet.

"I messed up," Adam blurted. "It's been a week and she won't see me or even take my calls. I've been to her apartment. I know she's there, yet she won't come to the door. Every day I send her flowers and candy, but she refuses delivery. I'm screwed. She really meant it when she said she didn't want to see me again."

"Did you two do it?" J.R. blurted out.

Adam leveled a stare which let J.R. know he didn't appreciate the question.

"Look, I'm just asking because ever since Star came from Mia's yesterday she's been acting funny, too."

"What did she say?"

"She kept babbling on about how precious life is and you have to cherish each moment. But she never directly said anything about what they talked about. I tried, man, but she wasn't giving it up. My take is this. One, you obviously did something that embarrassed her, or two, you let her embarrass herself." He plugged in the cable in the back and pressed the power button. Nothing happened. J.R. looked up.

"Which is it?"

Adam leaned his head back and shoved his hands in his pocket. "I let her embarrass herself," he mumbled, and winced when J.R. slapped him between the shoulders, laughing loudly.

"Don't look so sad, homey. It's your fault, but I'm your ticket to redemption."

"What are you talking about?" Adam demanded, in no mood for games.

"Just be at Pops' tomorrow night at seven o'clock. I'll take care of the rest."

Sparks shot from the back of the system and J.R. cursed, jumping back. He snatched the plugs out and stared at it, a disgusted look on his face.

He jumped off the platform and walked toward the door of the studio. "I hope you know something about wiring, because the next class starts at two o'clock."

Adam consulted his watch and began pulling cables from the powerful system, smiling.

Adam swung the garment bag onto the overstuffed chair and stared out the bay window, wondering if his life would ever be peaceful again.

His conversation with Lester Walker earlier that day had proved fruitless. Candice had spun her web around her father too tight. He wouldn't believe anything he'd had to say.

But this business trip could change his life. He was as prepared as he could be to meet the one and only Dorian Thibedeaux.

Gathering his bags, Adam walked downstairs to the foyer. The comfort of the house surrounded him. Only one thing would make it perfect. If only Mia were at his side.

Falling in love wasn't easy. He found that out yesterday when he blew J.R.'s speakers out in the aerobics studio. He'd been thinking of seeing Mia again, and not concentrating.

He could see her in this house, with their children, happy and in love. He had to make it happen.

Loud music and voices greeted him as the limousine pulled up to the house on the south side of Atlanta.

"Driver, I'll be ready at eleven-thirty sharp," Adam said, and got out.

Friends and neighbors gathered outside the familiar house, smoking, playing cards, and visiting with each other.

Pops was the host of hosts as he talked to each of the guests, making sure everyone had something to drink and no one was doing anything illegal.

He saw Adam and burst into raucous laughter, catching him in a bear hug.

Unashamed of his affection for the older man, Adam kissed Pops on the cheek and slung his arm affectionately over his shoulder. Shorter than Adam by a head and a half, he was still a commanding presence as his loud voice carried over the crowd.

"The prodigal son has returned," he roared, and allowed Adam to be swept into the crowd of old friends.

Many of the familiar faces Adam had seen recently at his mother's funeral, but many more were there who couldn't make it, for whatever reason. Hugs and kisses were passed around and he caught up on the latest gossip about who was having babies, who had died or moved away.

Dandling babies of old girlfriends on his knees, he talked to them, laughing at the good memories yet knowing he had chosen the right road by pursuing his dream, and owning his own business.

Adam winked when he saw Star. "Where's your girlfriend?" he asked when they got close enough to talk.

"She'll be here," she assured.

Two hours passed, but he was completely aware of the moment when she arrived. His conversation drifted as he watched each step she took, the rise and fall of her chest and the slight sway of her hips when she walked.

Her bright, white, strapless dress fit like skin at the top, then flared at her hips. Heeled strapless sandals covered her feet and her hair was crimped into a funky style, lifting full around her head.

Adam devoured her with his eyes in a matter of seconds, wanting to approach her, yet staying in his seat. She was too nervous. Too tentative. Even after that night. Somewhere deep inside her was a passionate woman dying to come out. He was determined to help her release her.

Mia's smile brightened when she spotted J.R. and Star, and she giggled as she was introduced and led away by Pops.

"Who's that girl?" Mrs. Herrington asked as they sat side by side in the shadows on the porch.

"That's my future wife."

Mrs. Herrington nodded, patting his hand. "Then go get her."

Adam stretched his long legs and stood. He approached Pops from behind and dropped his hand on his shoulder.

"Mia, here's my other boy. Adam, where you been? I was looking for you earlier. Sit down and have some fish and meet Mia. Mia, this is my other son, Adam. Adam, Mia."

Staring at the couple, Pops looked from one to another when neither spoke. "Boy, where are your manners? Speak to the girl. Sit down." Grumbling about manners and young people, Pops walked away to go turn more fish and serve new guests.

Adam straddled the picnic bench, next to Mia, who sat with her hands laced on her lap. "I've missed you," he said, and tweaked a lock of hair. "I'm sorry," he whispered in her ear, hoping she would respond. She sighed and tilted her head toward him. He grazed his nose against her cheek until she cupped his face and looked at him.

"Move closer," he whispered. "Show me that I'm not crazy for how I feel about you." A low chuckle broke from him as she slid an inch closer to him.

"A little more," he urged, watching her slim hips come another fraction of an inch nearer. Unable to resist any longer, he laced his hands together on the other side of her waist. His powerful legs propelled him forward as her hips came to rest between his legs.

Mia put her hands on his chest. "It was all my fault. You don't have anything to be sorry for. And the roses are beautiful."

Adam nudged her again. And again. And again. He kept
doing it until he had her smiling and squirming in her seat. He
took her hand and helped her from the bench. They strolled
out of the yard and stopped by a huge willow tree several
houses away.

He pulled her into his arms. "Why wouldn't you take my
calls? At first, I thought I did something to hurt you."

"I wasn't hurt. I—" She hesitated, then continued in a
whisper, her fingers tracing his breastbone. "I wanted you, too.
I'm embarrassed to say this but, uh, well, it's been a while for
me. And I didn't know what to do. Then I got confused about
whether I should be there, and what you would think of me in
the morning type thoughts."

He laughed and she cringed, pushing away from him.

"Don't—," he said holding her tight. "Stop pushing me
away." Their foreheads touched and he looked at her, the love
in his heart bursting. "I would love to have you in my bed in
the morning. To see you the day after, and after that, would
make me very happy. Baby, there's something between us
that's growing every day." Mia felt it, too, and wriggled closer.

"I felt strange. Things I've never felt before," she gasped
in his ear, wrapping her arms around his neck. "It's not just
sex. Is it?"

"No," he said, hoarsely.

"How much of me do you want, Adam? I need to know. I
don't want to hurt you by not being able to give you more than
I have."

Adam crushed her to him, his mouth claiming hers hungrily.
He tried to leave his desire imprinted on her soul as he delved
deep within her mouth. His demanding lips caressed hers, and
he lifted her off her feet. When he lowered her and broke away,
their breathing was choppy and uneven.

His voice was raspy when he came up for air.

"That's how I want you. Every day. All the time. Don't
ever be embarrassed. And you don't have to be sorry." Adam

ran his fingers down her sides, watching her eyes spark with desire.

"I want you to feel everything you can that's beautiful and fun. What we were doing was beautiful. It doesn't matter if we're on the couch, or in the bed or even in the shower or on the floor. I don't care, as long as we're together."

He laughed at her breathlessness. "You and I are going to be together. You're the one right thing I have in my life. Nothing about you is a lie or fake, and if it takes fifty years I'll wait."

He nipped her ear and she made a purring sound. "Was it good?" he asked, his hands roaming up her sides.

Her fingers fluttered, stroking his neck.

"It was better than good," she whispered. "It was heaven."

He kissed her again. "That good?" he questioned.

"That good."

"I wish we were somewhere else right now," Adam said unsteadily, his heart threatening to burst out of his chest. They calmed down, and he took her hand, leading her back to the yard.

Adam relaxed, enjoying the rest of the cookout because Mia was at his side. They talked, and every once in a while, when he thought no one was looking, he sneaked a kiss.

The evening flew by, and he watched her charm Pops so that the older man was putty in her hands.

"How did you get here?" he asked after they finished their fish dinner.

"I rented a car. I meant to ask you where my car was. I sent the tow truck to pick it up and he said it was gone."

J.R. walked up behind them, tickling her. "The wrecker offered me fifty dollars for it and I took it."

"J.R.! Quit." She squirmed, laughing. "You better not have sold my car." Mia turned back to Adam.

"Where is it?"

"It's in the shop." She opened her mouth and he cut her off. "I tried to call you, but somebody wasn't taking my calls.

Remember?'' Her mouth snapped shut. ''So I called my mechanic and he's having a look at it.''

''I can't afford that. Just tell him to have it towed back to my house.''

''So what are you going to do for a ride? I can't come by your house and drive you to work every day. Besides, J.R. needs me to drive him, too,'' Star interrupted, rolling her eyes at them.

They all laughed at her exaggeration. ''I don't know.'' Mia shrugged. ''But tonight I have a ride, so we won't worry about it.''

''You can take my car,'' Adam offered. He dug in his pocket and pulled out his key ring. ''J.R., take her to the house and give her Mom's car. It's just sitting there going to waste.''

''No. Really, thank you, but I'll manage. You don't have to do that.''

Star butted in again. ''I can't drive you.''

''And the bus doesn't run in your county,'' J.R. added.

''And rental cars must be at least fifty dollars a day,'' Adam added convincingly.

''Okay! Okay. I'll drive the darn thing.'' She snatched the keys from his hand and sat back down. They all stared at her, then burst out laughing.

''Now that's the Mia I know,'' J.R. said as he and Star walked over to join Pops.

The limousine pulled up in front of the house. Adam slowly walked toward it, taking Mia's hand.

''I'll only be gone for three weeks. I hope.''

''You mean it might be longer?''

''Yeah.'' He signaled the driver to stay in the car. ''It depends on how well things go.''

''Good luck. I know this is very important to you.''

''You're important to me, too.'' His eyes slid over her appreciatively.

He leaned against the car and crossed his arms.

"I can only ask you this while I'm not touching you," he said, his eyes dancing.

Mia started to grin. "What is it?"

"Do you have on anything beneath that top?"

She tilted her head to the side, her lips curved. Adam groaned when she pulled out the front of her top and looked down. "Mmm, I don't see anything. Maybe you could help—. Oh, I do see something there."

She let it snap against her skin just as he reached for her. "I'm not wearing anything."

"Mia Jacobs, when I get my hands on you—"

"Sir, we have to leave now, or you're going to miss that red-eye." The limousine driver cut in just as he planted a wet kiss on her neck.

"One more minute," he ground out, his lips barely leaving her.

"Give me something to come home to, baby." Music and laughter swirled around them, but neither was aware. Each focused on the magnetism of their desire.

His mouth burned a fiery path past her ear and over her cheek until he found what was close to his destination. Her fingers sidetracked him and slipped across his lips. He captured two of them, sucking them in.

Mia stepped into his stance, pressing against him, making him so hard he thought he would burst. Adam grasped her palm, pulling her fingers from his mouth, and claimed her parted lips with greedy desire.

Reluctantly, he pulled away as good sense prevailed. It was a struggle for control he didn't want to yield to, but he finally took his hands off her for a moment.

"Help me somebody, I'm about to get arrested . . ." Adam groaned when they broke away. Voices neared, and a couple passed on their way up the street.

"Mmm?" she said when he pulled her back within his embrace.

"I'm going to make love to you in the street. I'm sure that's a crime against somebody. Not me," he assured.

Mia backed away from him, a tiny smile on her face. Their eyes held for a moment, then she waved. "Go. You don't want to miss your plane."

"Come with me to Hawaii," he said, reaching out to her.

For a moment she seemed to consider it, the way she stared at his outstretched hand. Her eyes met his, and she giggled nervously.

"Hawaii? Hawaii?" she said. "I can't. No, I have to work."

The driver got out and opened the door for him. Adam slid into the seat and closed the door. He rolled down the window.

"I'll see you in a few weeks," Mia said as the car rolled up the street.

"I'll miss you," he said.

To his surprise, she touched her hand to her lips and blew him a kiss. He didn't know if she was aware of what she said, but he heard her as clear as if she were whispering in his ear. It sustained him for five grueling days when he worked around the clock and couldn't talk to her.

He was sure she said she loved him, too.

Chapter 14

"J.R., it's Adam, get up. How's Mia?"

"Do you know what time it is?" J.R. grumbled into the phone.

Adam could hear Star fussing. Then the phone fell, and a loud thud boomed through the phone lines.

"Man, this had better be important. She just kicked me out of the bed."

"Go to the office. I'm faxing you pictures of the flowers I think would go with Star's dress. You should get this any minute." J.R.'s desk chair squeaked, so Adam knew when he got there. The fax machine began to hum in the background.

"I got it," J.R. said. "Man, these are nice."

Adam rubbed his weary eyes and leaned back on the bed. The exotic beauty of the islands, the sandy beaches and stunning sunsets were lost on him. All conference rooms looked alike, once you'd been in enough of them.

He still hadn't gotten accustomed to the six hour time difference between Atlanta and Hawaii. The round-the-clock negotiations with Thibedeaux were taking their toll.

It didn't help that he wasn't even guaranteed the contract.

That was the frustrating part. Then being away from Mia, that was too much.

"How is she?"

"Mia's fine. Why don't you call yourself and quit buggin' me? I bet she's asleep, Adam, 'cause we're asleep," J.R. said sarcastically. "Can't a brother get some rest?"

"You woke yet?" Adam asked once J.R. quit whining.

"Yes," he sighed. "What is it?"

"Is she okay?"

"Really, man, she's fine. She looks good sportin' Grace's car. Call her."

"Yeah, I think I will," he said, stifling a yawn.

"You sound as tired as I am. Is it going okay?"

Adam looked for the floral bedspread, which was buried under a mountain of discarded proposals and presentations. The one he finally selected had been the most comprehensive and concise of them all. He had done his homework. All he needed now was some luck.

"I think so," he finally said.

"Well then, my bed is calling."

"Okay. Kiss Star for me. I'll see you in a couple of weeks. Later."

Adam shrugged out of his shirt and tie, trading them for running shorts and sleeveless T-shirt. He took a forty minute run on the beach to burn his final energy so that he could sleep. Exhausted after his shower, he lay nude on the cool sheets and dialed the phone.

The ringing phone set her into action as she shut off the water to the shower. Snatching the towel, Mia hurried to answer it before it split the early morning quiet again.

"Hi Mia, it's Mom."

"What's going on, Mom? It's five o'clock your time."

Mia sat on the edge of the bed and slid her exercise shorts on while cradling the phone between her shoulder and ear. She hurried to the kitchen counter and wrapped a bagel in plastic wrap before returning to the bed.

Suddenly, she stopped moving.

"It's about Nikki," her mother said. "The Chicago police questioned Derrick about Nikki's death."

Mia's heart pounded. "Why? What do they have to do with anything?"

"He got arrested for something here. Hold on. Your father knows." Mia heard her mother start to cry, and fear she wanted to ignore raced through her veins. "I'm sorry this happened. I'm so sorry."

"Mia, you there?" Retired detective sergeant Mason Jacob's voice sounded grim.

"Yes sir," she responded automatically.

"This could all be a bunch of hogwash. I got this information second-hand, but I still have strong connections in the Chicago Police Department. From what I hear, the district attorney just handed down indictments on five of the lawyers in the firm Derrick worked for. They've been charged with taking insider trading information and acting on it personally. Derrick passed the information on to others, which is how they got busted.

"Apparently he bragged to one of the undercover agents about having some involvement in Nikki's death. I don't know more than that."

His words rocked her. Mia held her head between her knees, her mind whirling.

"Nobody told me if they have proof on tape or what exactly was said. So don't get your hopes up. Yet."

Mia couldn't connect the shallow breathing as her own. It was just too hard to believe. She had suspected him, but to hear that her suspicions might be true was too hard to fathom.

"Dad," she said hoarsely. "Call me the minute you hear anything. I—I need to know."

His voice softened to an accustomed gentleness. It touched a soft spot in her.

"I wish I could have called and said we caught him straight-

away, but I can't. We called now because we didn't want you
to hear from somewhere else that they may have something on
him.''

"Yes sir," she said quietly.

"We're going to get him. Do you hear me, Mia? It's just a
matter of time before we do. I'll make sure of that."

"Thanks," was all she could manage.

"Mia?" Her mother's voice came on the line, shaky and
tear-filled.

"Ma'am?"

"Be good. We love you."

Mia lowered the phone, willing the painful ache away.

"I knew it. I knew it. Oh God, help me . . ." she cried,
giving in to the grief. Guilt tore through her with the savagery
of a knife. She cried for her child and herself, placing the blame
squarely on her own shoulders.

*I should have been there. I should have been able to save
her.*

The phone bleated an agitated sound, and she fumbled, hanging it up. Mia dried her eyes, avoiding looking at herself as
she washed her face. Her hiccups rang out in the silent room,
and she forced them down until they stopped.

Mia finished dressing and picked up the bagel, then dropped
it in the trash, disgusted at the thought of eating.

She walked around the small room with jerky, stilted steps.
Somehow she made it out the door. It stuck as she tried to lock
it, the key refusing to turn in the lock. One slow tear splashed
off her cheeks and she wiped it, the cool wind making her face
colder.

Her unbound hair whipped in her face, and she gave up her
fight with the door. Mia rolled her eyes and stopped for a
moment to wipe the tears from her face. Robotically, she walked
back inside for a jacket and hair bow, then locked the door
without a problem.

The engine of the Lexus hummed to life, so unlike her car,

which she hardly missed. Her thoughts flew to Adam as she sat behind the wheel allowing it time to warm up.

He hadn't called even once, and she questioned what she was to him. Probably nothing. The car smoothly accepted the shift into reverse and she drove out of the parking lot, missing the ringing phone in her apartment.

Chapter 15

"Mia, where are you? I miss you . . ." Adam's mellow baritone was edged with concern as it floated through her answering machine.

Snatching it, she sank to the floor. "Adam," she called, her own voice huskier than usual.

"I'm here. Let me cut the machine off." Her heart raced as his delighted chuckle rippled through the phone lines.

"How are you?"

"I'm fine, baby. How are you?"

"I'm okay," she said too quickly. "How's business? Have you found what you were looking for?"

Every fiber of her body tingled at his chuckle. It held soft intimate promises, and she was ready to succumb to them. She missed him, and she needed him, more than she ever could admit.

"Only you." His words sank in, hitting home. "Woman, where have you been? Is J.R. working you too hard? Because I can take care of him, like I used to," he teased.

"No." She sighed, hoping the loneliness she felt didn't seep into her voice. "I took over a few classes for this week and it's been kind of hectic. But a good hectic," she said cheerily. "I've had a bit of free time on my hands, so I didn't mind."

The silence from the other end was deafening.

"Don't make me fly home tomorrow, because you're not telling me the truth."

"No." Her voice dropped as she cradled the phone, climbing into her bed.

"There's a flight in two hours," he warned, and she could hear the determination in his voice.

"Okay, okay," she said, sighing heavily. "It's hard to talk about," she said, then poured her heart out about Derrick and his suspected involvement in Nikki's death. She didn't stop for an hour, and when she did it was because she was exhausted.

"So when my parents called this morning, that was the final straw. I blame myself. I should have been there."

"Don't, baby," he said softly. "You can't torture yourself with what should have happened. It won't help. It won't change anything."

"Do you ever wish you could start a day over?"

"Don't do that, Mia. I know how you feel, but you can't go back."

"I know. It's finally hitting me that I have to move on."

"I'm coming home Friday."

"You are? Are you done?"

"I will be." His steely determination raced through her. "I'll see you Friday. Mia?"

"Mmm?"

"Do you miss me?"

Silence hung between them. "Yes, I do."

The roar of the silence crackled with his appreciative laughter.

"I'll be home Friday. Will you meet me at the airport? I'll be in at four o'clock."

Mia had been waiting to hear this, and she controlled her relief that he was coming home.

"I'll meet you," she answered, somewhat breathless.

"Good. I'll be so glad to see you. Catch the train, okay? I've already got a car ordered."

"I'll be there."

Another hour passed as they continued to talk, neither eager to hang up. He muffled a yawn.

"Adam, we've been on the phone forever. This has to be expensive."

"You're worth every cent. But you're right. I do have a meeting to get prepared for. Keep your fingers crossed. Hopefully, it'll be the last."

"Adam," she called before he hung up.

"Yes, baby?" She got such a thrill when he called her that.

"I miss you, too. Goodnight."

Mia replaced the receiver and fell back on the floor.

She had made it through another day.

I'm falling in love. The thought rocketed her out of the bed and onto her feet. Memories of Adam's soothing voice and sexy smile swam in front of her.

Love wasn't good. It hurt, it ended and it died.

Going alone to the airport was a bad idea. Mia picked up the phone and dialed.

"Star, it's Mia. Didn't you want to discuss the wedding arrangements this week? Well I need you to do me a favor—"

Mia explained everything, and when she was done, she felt a real sense of accomplishment.

Friday came too quickly. As she prepared to go to Hartsfield International Airport, the uneventful train ride gave her an opportunity to review her plan and check for problems.

Seeing none, Mia relaxed against the seat, trying to anticipate his reaction. A crowd was certainly not what he would expect, especially the one she had planned for him.

She smiled despite herself, tickled at her ingenuity. If she kept Adam with a crowd of people, they wouldn't have the time, nor the opportunity, to get too personal.

She alighted the train and spotted J.R. and Star on the platform. "Hey, guys?" she greeted warmly.

"J.R. did you bring him a change of clothes?" Mia couldn't stop her babbling, and snapped her lips shut when she noticed how strangely J.R. was looking at her.

"What are you so hyped for? It's just us. Adam hasn't ever had this type of recep—" He eyed her suspiciously.

"Does Adam know we're here to pick him up?"

Mia ignored him and studied the television monitors. "He's coming through the International Concourse. Come on, let's go." Dragging Star with her, she avoided J.R. but was snagged by him at the gate.

The already disembarking passengers streamed out of the tunnel as she craned her head to see.

"Answer me . . . aw hell," J.R. said. He reached out but was too slow for Star, who jumped up and down, waving.

Mia slipped into the crowd when she spotted Adam's head in the tunnel. He was impossible to miss. The low fade and tiny curls stood out amongst the contrasting blonde heads and tanned faces that were around him.

He had gotten some sun. It enhanced his dark features, making then glow. As he neared them he seemed to have grown taller, and he looked good, even though he sported airplane wrinkles on his suit.

Excitement surged through her, and Mia tried to tamp it down as Adam laid his garment bag on the ground by J.R.'s feet.

Star stared between her and Adam, then at J.R., her face a mask of confusion. Reality finally hit her. "You set us up, you little sneak," she said, poking Mia in the arm.

"You weren't expecting us, were you?" she said to Adam.

Adam's eyes locked with Mia's. She felt as if she'd been let off a roller coaster ride when he dropped his gaze to Star. "I'm happy to see you," he said, and planted a brotherly kiss on Star's cheek, then shook J.R.'s hand.

"Mia."

Her name came out as a husky whisper, and she gravitated toward him. His hands were warm and more calloused than she remembered, but they felt so good against hers. How could she forget? she wondered fleetingly when they stood inches apart.

His gaze was riveted to hers. Slowly it lingered, then settled back on her face as soft as a caress.

"Welcome home," she said, kissing him on the cheek.

Adam pressed her against him until her breasts crushed into his chest. "Oh, I know you can do better than that, can't you?"

Blood rushed to her face via her toes, and she wound her arms around his neck. She didn't care anymore that they were in the middle of the airport, or that their friends were watching, grinning like silly fools.

All that mattered was that he kiss her, and soon.

Mia was shocked at her eager response to the touch of his lips, but the demanding kiss unleashed passion she didn't know lived in her. Adam groaned in response and deepened the kiss, their tongues snaking each other's in a wild swirl.

She had somehow missed this fire in her life.

It was too good to end, but three lingering kisses later his mouth slid to her cheek, and Mia buried her head against his throat.

"Hello," he whispered into her ear. "I see why you brought company."

She stepped away and J.R. shoved a bag in Adam's arms.

"Go change, lover boy. We're *all* supposed to be having fun, right?"

"Is this fun, Jacobs style?"

Adam pretended to talk in her ear, instead taking little nips as the chauffeur driven limousine pulled up in front of the bowling alley.

"You don't want to bowl?" she asked, anxiety stealing her pleasant smile. The shield she used to protect herself slammed up. It had been that way the whole night. She smiled at the right time and said the right things, but her responses were forced, automatic.

J.R. and Star had already gotten out. He held her back. "Bowling is fine. I want to know what's going on. Did something else happen?" He watched her more closely, taking in the dark circles under her eyes and how tight her mouth was drawn.

She'd lost weight, too.

"Nothing happened," she said, pushing open the door. "Come on, let's go in."

"You can't keep running," he said after they got in line behind J.R. and Star.

Her eyes closed for a moment and her shoulders slumped.

When she turned, she met his gaze squarely. "I have to do what's best for me. Talking about every slice of drama in my life won't help. Now let's have some fun."

Her words ended in a plea. He wanted to comfort her, but how could he when she wouldn't reach out to him?

They followed J.R. once they got their bowling shoes.

It was league night, and large groups of people milled around lanes. Pins crashed, and, while some groups cheered, others threw towels, cursing.

"Had I known you were planning this evening's fun around a bowling alley, I would have brought my lucky ball," J.R. fussed. "As it is now, I have to bowl with alley trash." He handled the bowling alley balls like they were dead rodents.

Star and Adam chorused, "Shut up!" They lined up at the single lane, and Mia and Star dropped their purses on a bench so they could lace their shoes.

"You're still going to get beat," Adam goaded J.R., while keeping an eye on Mia. "Just like every other time when you *have* your ball. Tonight, you might even get lucky with one of these balls."

Adam walked to the racks. Mia passed him on the way to the rack, but didn't act as if she'd saw him.

"So I wouldn't complain if I were you," Adam concluded, keeping an eye on her.

J.R. decided the lineup and acted as the unofficial coach for everybody in the next two lanes. They enjoyed his good-natured friendliness. Otherwise, it would have been very quiet.

"Anybody hungry?" Star asked, digging through her purse for money.

"Not me," Mia said, picking up her ball for her turn to bowl. Adam was captivated by her every move. The way she held her hand over the blower, then inserted her fingers in the dark holes of the ball. The teeny, tiny baby steps she took, then the last big one.

Then gutter. It was hilarious when she stamped her feet, her hands pressed into her hips.

J.R. slapped his head, calling over his shoulder to Star as he walked up to Mia, "Get me some nachos. It's going to be a long night."

Adam took a long pull on his beer and shook his head as J.R. demonstrated another of his famous, fail-proof bowling tips to Mia.

He was unaware of Star's presence until the box she carried brushed his leg. He helped her unload the box, and left it in the back so the workers could dispose of it.

"Do you love her?"

Star stood beside him, peering at him.

He nodded. "I can't stop thinking about her. She haunts my dreams when I sleep, and when I'm awake I still dream about her. When I was away these last few weeks, at night I would reach for her and wake up cold and frustrated that she wasn't there. I feel like I'm the only man in the world who can feel this way. I love her."

Star beamed. "You deserve it after you know who."

He pushed Candice into the recesses of his mind. Thinking of her selfish habits made him angry. It had taken too long to get home to dampen everything with thoughts of her.

Adam squeezed Star's shoulder, thankful for her support.

"Mia's very delicate. I have to take my time and show her."
He voiced his worry. "Something's going on, though."

The pins at the end of the alley exploded in a strike and Mia
jumped, screaming.

She came back, cheering, then wrapped her arms around his
waist. Her chin rested on his shoulder and he touched his head
to hers.

This was the way he liked them. Natural. Comfortable.

J.R. changed his order again. "I'll have eggs, bacon, toast
and waffles. No, make that hash browns," he wavered. Then
he decided. "Just bring it all."

Mia rolled her eyes, glad that he had finally finished. She
glanced out the window at where Adam stood talking to the
limousine driver.

Her stomach clutched again and she held it, wishing the pain
would go away.

"Is he this difficult all the time?" she asked Star after J.R.
excused himself from the table.

"Naw," she said with a toss of her auburn head. "He's
better." Mia caught the double meaning and laughed.

"You love him, don't you Star?"

A rush of loneliness crept over her when a vibrant smile
graced Star's face, making her cheeks flame.

"I love him crazy. That's why we want to have the wedding
so soon. We want to start having our children—"

"Mia!"

Mia heard her name in the distance, and her stomach gripped
tight again. She couldn't answer Star, and she wanted to say
she was all right, but hot bile rose in her throat, blocking her
words. Her eyes stung, and her ears rang until finally she began
the downward slide.

"Oh," she said once, then black oblivion.

* * *

"I didn't mean to upset her . . ." Star cried against J.R.'s chest. Adam frantically tried to stop the bleeding from the nasty gash on Mia's forehead.

He had seen her falling like a limp rag doll, but she had already banged her head on the table before he could get to her. He didn't know if she had any other injuries because of how she lay.

"Mia, wake up," he said, shaking her.

Her dark lashes lay against her cheeks like long black caterpillars. She didn't move.

Desperately, Adam felt for a pulse. It was strong and consistent, but she was still unconscious.

"Somebody call an ambulance," he ordered, and dragged off his jacket. He covered her with it, then pressed his blood-soaked handkerchief into her forehead, praying.

He couldn't lose her, too.

"Talk to her," J.R. said after he quieted Star. "Maybe if she hears your voice she'll come around."

Adam nodded and began to speak softly in her ear. "Sweetheart, can you hear me? Everything is going to be okay." Her unresponsiveness shook him, and he feared there might be injuries he couldn't see. "Please wake up, baby. I need you," he whispered.

His pleas swam into her unconsciousness like cool ocean water. It lapped at her, then rushed away. It kept coming until it surrounded her, lifting her up in a gentle rocking motion, reminding her of the first time she was in his arms.

Adam was the protection, the safety, she needed. He was the love she wanted.

She slid closer to his voice.

"Mia, open your eyes.

"She's coming around. J.R., give me your jacket. She's cold. Mia, can you hear me? The ambulance is here. You're going to be fine. Open your beautiful eyes, baby."

For a brief second her lids fluttered, then slid up. She blinked twice before they closed again.

"J.R., she opened her eyes."

There was movement from everywhere. Adam could feel the pressure on his arm from the paramedic.

He moved, giving them access to her, but watched intently as they performed a preliminary examination.

Unspeakable pressure built in his chest as he kneeled helplessly beside her.

"She's fighting," the paramedic said. "Hold her down."

Her eyes flew open and she clenched his hand with surprising strength. She moaned, moving her head from side to side as panic filled her eyes.

"I'm okay," she mumbled, her speech slurred. "Adam, I'm okay."

"Sorry, Miss. You're coming with us. Sir, you have to move so we can get the gurney in."

Adam moved long enough for them to slide her on, then was back at her side. The death grip she kept on his hand scared him, and her pleas broke his heart.

"I can't go back. Don't make me."

"Mia, they want to help you. I'll go with you. I won't let anyone hurt you. Do you hear me?" he said urgently. "I won't let anyone hurt you . . .

"What's happened to her!" Adam yelled at the paramedics as the ambulance raced toward the Emergency Center.

"She's in shock. They deal with this all the time. Don't worry sir, they can handle this type."

Time stopped for him as she was unloaded and taken into the hospital. Her eye was nearly covered with white gauze, and the hand that once gripped his was now limp.

An intruding voice interrupted his thoughts.

"Sir, do you know when she ate last?"

"No."

"Name?" the nurse asked.

"Mia Jacobs."

"Age?"

"I don't know."

"Address?"

He completed it, stumbling over the zip code.

"Next of kin?"

"I don't know."

"Blood type?"

"Don't know."

"Last period?"

"Huh?"

The list of questions went on forever. The more the nurse asked, the less he knew. The woman he loved was a complete mystery to him.

Finally he was ushered in the room where she lay, pale but conscious. Sad tears streamed from her eyes when she saw him, but she smiled. Seeing it did his heart good, and he wrapped her in a fierce embrace.

"You gave me quite a scare out there," he murmured, tenderly stroking her hair over the white bandages. It was tangled and matted in places where blood had dried.

"I'm sorry."

"For once it's good to hear you say that." He dried her tearstained face.

"Excuse me, Mr. Jacobs, we need you to sign some papers for your wife. They state you will be responsible for payment . . ." Adam nodded and motioned for the pen. Grabbing it, he scribbled his signature, his eyes never leaving her face.

"Excuse me, he's—" Mia said weakly.

He pressed his finger to her lips. "Where is the doctor?" Adam asked over his shoulder.

"He'll be right with you."

Mia lay back and slipped into a quiet sleep. The mild sedative they had given her to calm her down had taken effect. Adam had time to focus on what had happened, and he was completely confused.

He prayed that it wasn't serious. He thought of his mother and her valiant fight with cancer, and the loss of her in his life. He didn't know if he could handle something like that again.

Gently he stroked her cheek and she roused, tears streaming from her eyes.

"Mia, what is it? You're breaking my heart, sweetheart, because I don't know how to make you feel better."

"I want to go home," she said and he cradled her to him.

"Soon. The doctor will be here to check you out and then we can leave. Do you hurt anywhere, do you need anything?" Adam couldn't stop touching her. He wanted her all in one piece.

"Just you next to me." His hands climbed up her arms, pulling her close. They stayed that way until the doctor entered the room. His exam ended quickly and he picked up her chart and reviewed it.

"She's got to drink something before we can release her. By all indications her head is going to be okay. Her blood pressure is down, though, and her body is empty. By the looks of her eyes, she hasn't had much sleep either.

"She's dehydrated and malnourished. Keep her quiet for a few days. No strenuous activity."

Adam looked up, catching his unspoken message.

"She needs rest," the doctor continued, "but wake her every two hours, asking her these questions."

He handed Adam a list and juice. "She also needs to make an appointment so we can look at that bump on her head in one week. Her blood results will arrive by mail in a few days. We only call if something is out of the norm. Good luck."

"Thank you," Adam said, and the doctor left the room.

"Did you hear that, Mia? We can go just as soon as you drink this juice. When was the last time you ate?"

"I don't know," she said hoarsely. "I haven't been hungry."

Probably since she got the news of her ex-husband's potential involvement in the death of their daughter.

Hot anger rushed through him, and he swore if he ever got his hands on the man he would make him very sorry for hurting her.

The nurse helped her dress, and he slipped away to call a cab. "Are you ready?" he asked when he came back to the room.

"I'm ready," she said weakly.

Adam drew her against him as the cab whipped through the quiet streets.

They dozed until the wheel bumped the curb of his driveway, shaking him awake. He had never been so glad to see his house before, as the cab curved around the driveway.

Adam stifled a yawn while paying the driver. He helped Mia up the stairs to his room, where he gave her one of his pajama shirts, and some privacy to change.

"You're so nice to me," she said when he came back in the room to check on her. Turning, she nestled into the huge, down-filled comforter and fell sound asleep.

A lump filled his throat as he watched her shallow breathing. Her dark hair fanned out over the black pillowcase. The white bandage stood out against it.

The shrill ring startled him. He sprinted to the phone, trying to catch it before it could wake her.

"Hello?"

"Is she okay, man?" J.R.'s voice was filled with worry.

"She'll be fine," Adam said contritely, remembering he was supposed to call. "We just got here. She has to rest, and no strenuous activity for a few days."

"Hey man, no problem. She doesn't have to worry about work. She's been bustin' her butt teaching everybody's classes lately. We owe her some time off. Tell her we love her."

"I will," Adam responded, looking across the room at Mia, who had curled into a ball in the center of the bed.

"Call if you need us. Peace."

"Peace."

Jet lagged and tired, Adam showered and changed in the guest bathroom. He returned to his room, laden with pillows and blankets. He resisted crawling in beside her.

Instead, he stretched out on the couch in the living room of his suite. Before he passed out from exhaustion, he set the clock for exactly two hours.

Adam sat in the chair beside his bed and watched Mia sleep. She stretched, and kicked off the thick comforter, exposing a shapely bottom and thigh.

With great care not to wake her, Adam repositioned the covers and took up a new place at the window. He needed distance between them because seeing her half dressed, wearing his clothes, was having a murderous effect on his control.

Adam drew his hands down over his face, his two day growth of whiskers scratching them. He stared out over the gardens and didn't see them. His work was impossible, as was sleep.

How could he let her know his feelings without scaring her off? He loved her, that was for sure. But could she accept it?

"Adam, are you in here?"

"I'm right here," he said, staying at the window. "Do you need something for the pain?"

"No," she said after clearing her throat. She smoothed her hair down, her fingers tangling in the ends. She winced and held her forehead.

"Why did a freight train run over my head?" Her glazed eyes searched for him. He sat in the chair beside the bed.

She settled against the pillow, his nightshirt falling open at the curve of her breast. He made himself answer without drawing a path down her cleavage with his finger.

"I don't know exactly," he said, taking her hand. "One minute you were talking to Star, and the next you were on the floor with a bump on your head, compliments of the table at the Waffle House."

"I remember," she murmured. "I appreciate everything you've done for me."

"Shhh. You don't have to thank me."

She glanced at him, then down at their hands. Her inner struggle played on her face, and he wondered what she was thinking.

"Why don't you get some rest," he suggested, half rising. "We can talk later."

Mia scooted to the middle of the bed.

"Will you stay?"

Chapter 16

The sound of running water filtered into his dreams as Adam slept. He stretched, reaching for Mia, but she wasn't there. He sat up abruptly. Had it all been a dream?

The water went off, and his blood raced into overdrive when Mia came out of the bathroom.

His deep green bath towel stopped midthigh and he had an unencumbered view of long, shapely legs. She stopped halfway between the bed and bathroom, when she realized he was watching.

Adam lowered his feet to the floor, but kept his eyes on her.

"I borrowed your shower," she said.

"Do you feel better?"

They both spoke at the same time, then fell silent.

"You need to eat," he said quietly.

"I really need clothes," she said, smiling, smoothing her wet hair. "And a blow dryer would help, too. And a comb and toothbrush, too."

"You look good just the way you are." Adam crossed to the door, his hand on the knob. "I'll be back in a few minutes."

He found what she needed, then left her alone.

Don't touch her, he kept telling himself. He showered in the guest bathroom, taking an extra five minutes under the cold water. It was supposed to ease the ache in his groin. But every time he thought of her half dressed in his bath towel . . . He didn't want to think about it.

Adam shut off the water, traded his towel for running shorts and T-shirt, and headed toward the kitchen to whip up a fast breakfast. Every cabinet door was open as he searched for breakfast food. Eventually, he carried a tray up the stairs with his smorgasbord.

"You're looking better," he said, then grimaced. "Not that you looked bad before . . ."

"I hope that feast is for me?" she said lightly.

"Of course. I whipped up some scrambled eggs, chicken noodle soup, toast, juice . . ."

"Who's the bacon, grits and hash browns for?" she cut in, a teasing look crossing her face.

"Me," he said. "I haven't eaten since before I boarded that plane."

Adam set the tray down and she scooted over, making room for him. Adam scooped some of his grits onto her plate and made sure she ate them.

They were almost through when he said, "Tell me why you're afraid of hospitals. I don't understand how a doctor can be afraid of hospitals."

"I had taken Nikki to the hospital the day before she died because she had a mild cold. It was nothing serious, or I wouldn't have taken her to day care the next day. But her cold must have gotten worse. The school called my office and said she had a temperature.

"Only I didn't get the message until two hours later. By the time I got home, it was too late. The last place I saw her alive was the hospital."

She tore her toast into tiny shreds. "I guess I just had a bad reaction yesterday."

"So you quit your job?"

Mia tossed her braid over her shoulder. She rubbed her eyes

and stared out of the window as the evening sun faded. "I took a leave of absence. I have to go on," she said quietly.

It was the loneliest admission he'd ever heard.

"Not by yourself, you don't."

She simply shrugged.

Adam removed the breakfast tray, taking it to the kitchen. She had lain down in the bed, but the covers were held back to him in invitation. He slid in beside her and gathered her in his arms.

"Do you ever want to practice medicine again?"

"Yes, I do," she murmured, yawning, snuggling closer.

"I'm proud of you."

Mia draped her foot over his ankle, her even breath whispering in his ear.

"I love you, too," she said in her sleep.

It was late when she awoke, but the floodlights over the garden were bright, filtering through the blinds.

She knew that's where she would find Adam.

Following the cement path that wound through the fragrant bushes, she marveled again at the beauty and variety of the exquisite plants. The heady scent made her a little woozy, and she slowed her steps, fighting to keep her balance.

Adam kneeled elbow deep in rich pungent soil, just ahead. His strong dark back glistened from laboring as his gloved hands dug deep in the soil.

He worked quickly, potting bare branches.

Mia smiled as he cooed to the plants, talking to them as if they were people. He handled each one with a delicacy she had never known a man capable of.

"Adam."

Her tone must have triggered something in him, because he stripped off the long work gloves and came to her.

"What are you doing out here?" he asked, his eyes sliding over her.

"Looking for you," she said a little breathlessly. "I woke up and you were gone. "I—I'm much better." She stumbled over the words, knowing they were a lie. He was helping her heal. His love and patience was better than any pill or elixir.

"I should probably go home."

"I'm not going to let you go home and sit by yourself."

"Except—" she cut in.

"Tell me."

Desire propelled their lips together. Her face tingled from where he captured it in his hand, holding her in place so that her tongue could stroke his.

Adam lifted her, and she wrapped her legs around him as he carried her into the house and up the stairs to the center of his bed.

"Stay here," he said, taking her once again on a wild journey with his kiss. Mia fell back on the bed, anticipation eating at her. Within minutes he was back, clean and in shorts. His chest was bare. Mia reached for him, eager to feel his skin beneath her fingertips.

He palmed her face gently. "You know what's going to happen?" Adam nibbled her earlobe and slid his hands down her arms, twining their fingers. Her heart hammered when she responded.

"We're going to make love," she whispered.

"That's right," he said, and slid his hands beneath the shirt she wore. They covered her breasts, and her breath came in ragged gasps. Passion darkened his eyes, and she swam in the deep pools. When he pressured the tips she dropped her head to his shoulder, taking a small bite.

He groaned, his head falling back, and he grasped her hips, pulling them closer. Their mouths met again, the increased passion of knowing taking them higher.

His tongue danced with hers, drawing it out of her mouth, making hers follow, responding to the hunger that erupted from both.

Mia stepped back, gathering his long T-shirt in her hands.

She drew it up, pulling it over her head, wanting her hot skin to touch his. His extra large shorts hung off her hips, and she looked down at herself, seeing what he saw.

He growled, and it was the sexiest sound she'd ever heard. It clicked a valve in her, and she held her arms out to him.

Mia wanted him to touch her. She drew his hand up, placing it over her breast. But Adam didn't need direction. He knew just what she needed.

He lay her back and placed his mouth over the nipple. Mia cried out, his teeth and tongue driving her to unknown heights. His hands stroked the length of her thigh, grabbing her bottom with surprising strength. He wasn't gentle in the way he wanted her. It was hot, steamy, and demanding.

Mia loved the way he loved.

His mouth slid to her other breast and she bucked against him, capturing his head in her hands to keep him there. "I want you," she murmured in his ear.

Adam gave her what she asked for. His hands slid beneath her shorts and she gasped, calling his name when he stroked her sensitized nub.

That's when his touch gentled, teaching her the pleasures of her body. Shivers of delight shook her, and she flew close to something she had never known. Her nails dug into his arms when he rolled her on top of him, pressing her into his throbbing desire.

Adam grasped her to him and stopped moving.

"Adam, what happened?" she whispered, afraid that she had hurt him. "Did I do something wrong?"

"No," he groaned. *"I'm* doing something wrong. You're sick and I'm making love to you," he rasped into her hair. She could feel him still throbbing against her. He still wanted her.

Her hair had come unbound and blocked his face from view, and Mia sat up on top of him. It fell back, framing her face, as she swung it to one side before leaning over, placing soft kisses on his mouth and cheeks.

"Mia, get up. You're playing a dangerous game with a man who hasn't had any in a long time."

"Not longer than me, I bet," she said, taking little nips at his chin, running her hands lower.

"How long?" he rasped, his hands snaking up to catch hers as she tugged at the waist of his shorts. He ran his hands up the back of her shorts to grasp her bottom.

She whispered in his ear, "Three long years," and ground her hips into him. "I want to," she added.

Adam's control snapped.

He laid her down and stripped off her shorts. His followed, landing in a pile on the floor.

He suckled her breasts until they were raw from pleasure, and when his hands sought out the center of her desire, she was ready.

"Adam," she gasped, arching into him as he stroked her until her control began to slip. She tried to regain it, fighting the unknown pleasure. Mia squeezed tightly, her fingers and toes curling in her effort to stop the soaring her body demanded.

His fingers never stopped stroking as she mentally tried to distance herself from the pleasure. "Mia, let go," he urged, kissing her with an urgency she found thrilling.

"I can't . . . I never have," she said, burning all over.

She couldn't stop how her body responded to him, even though she was unsure of what lay ahead. When he slipped his fingers inside her, then touched her again, it was crazy that something could feel so good. His tongue slipped into her mouth.

Pleasure from everywhere blended together and burst.

It was delightful, ecstasy that sent her flying, until she was alone in the brilliance of passion. There was nothing better than this. She savored each blissful tremor, wishing she could slow the ride to make it last forever.

Adam held her throughout her orgasm, then slid on a condom before easing into her.

He set a slow rhythm, stirring the melting pot of desire. Mia opened wider for him, holding his sweat-slick back, panting, her release approaching.

When she flew over, it was with him harshly dragging out her name in his own release. There it was again. And she embraced the sweet oblivion.

Chapter 17

"What do you have for me?"

Behind the classic cedar desk, Star waited impatiently for the report to begin. Her impatience snapped. "Now, Jamal."

With a slightly lilting Jamaican accent, Jamal folded his hands over the manila folder, stalling.

"Star, I have to ask you, why you choose a boy to do a man's job? *I* am all the man you need." He grinned, showcasing a mouthful of yellowing teeth.

She knew he was referring to the fact that J.R. was a few years younger than she. Jamal apparently thought it was all right to discuss her personal life. He was dead wrong.

Star stood, her voice cold. "I hired you to do some investigative work for me. Not *about* me. If you ever do that again, let's just say that it's very hot back home in Jamaica, on the run."

The toothy smile disappeared.

Star was pleased. Her position in the Axial, a small government agency, afforded her certain information on everyone, even the investigators she hired to investigate for her. She was in the enviable position, depending on how you looked at it, of having anybody's information to her within hours.

She extended her hand. He slid the manila envelope into her palm. Star glanced at it, absorbed it, then reinserted the papers in the envelope. She sent it through the paper dicer. Jamal looked sick.

"Once again, your research is outstanding. Your money is in the same place. Goodbye."

She waited for him to leave her office before she picked up the phone and dialed.

"Adam, Star. Can I come over and talk to you? Great, see you in thirty minutes. Okay, two hours."

Mia was roused by Adam's moving to hang up the phone. She peered through her cracked eyelid to see that it was bright outside.

"It's daylight," she said, and flopped her head back on the bare mattress. She ran her fingers over the blue quilting, then up onto Adam's chest.

"Where are the sheets?" she asked.

"On the floor," he said, chuckling.

She shivered, in anticipation.

"Ooh, what's this?" she asked, gliding her hand up his hairy leg. He took her hand and closed it over himself. "I think you two have already met."

Mia lay tucked against Adam and watched the gold tips of the ceiling fan go around and around. He was in love with her. He hadn't said it, but she could feel it.

What would he expect from her? A family? *Definitely,* that annoying voice inside her warned.

Mia didn't want anything sad or miserable to ruin her bliss. She snuggled closer, closing her eyes.

Adam slid his thumb down the center of her back, telling her he was awake. "How old are you?"

"Thirty."

"Who's your next of kin?"

"What?" She giggled.

"Next of kin, tell me."

"My mother and father, Fiona and Mason Jacobs, of Chicago."

"Your last period?" She laughed as he tried to keep his own laughter down. She could hear it bubbling in his chest.

"I'm not telling you that," she said, tickling him.

"Any communicable diseases?"

"None," she replied, meeting his warm gaze.

"Me, either," he said.

"Good," she said.

"Good."

Mia woke up as Adam came out of the bathroom fully dressed. She had grown so accustomed to seeing him bare that clothes were an anomaly.

She sat up and swung her feet over the edge. "Stay there," he said softly. "You look good in my bed."

"I have to go home sometime." Mia picked up her discarded top and turned it right side out. Adam crossed the room and sat beside her, taking it from her hands.

"I have a meeting with Star. Then I thought we would eat. If you're ready to go after that, I'll take you." He lifted her chin until she looked into his eyes. "But I hoped you would stay. At least for tonight."

Mia wanted to cry. In the entire three days she'd spent with him she had gotten to know Adam, and it was impossible not to love him. He was sweet and kind and generous, and as far as she was concerned, even with her limited experience, the best lover on the planet.

"We'll talk when you get back," she said, touching her lips to his. "Give Star my love."

He gave her back her shirt. "I'll be back soon."

"How's Mia?" Star asked as she dropped her briefcase and purse in the armchair.

Adam watched as she paced the floor of the sunroom, her red curls bobbing as she walked.

"She's fine. She sends her love. What's the matter?"

She stopped pacing and faced him.

"Adam, please don't ask me how I know this or where I got the information from. As it is, I have no business knowing this, but you're my friend and I would never forgive myself for not warning you."

"Go on," he said grimly.

"Lester Walker has put in a bid on the Thunder stores in a takeover attempt."

Adam felt his chest tightening. "So he's going to buy them out and keep me from getting their business. Damn!"

"That isn't all. Apparently his wife, Eugenia, is back, too. They've been estranged for over ten years, and the company is still hers. He's just been running it. Although my information isn't confirmed, it's rumored that she bought controlling stock. It looks like she's planning to take him down."

"You mean to tell me that Walker's isn't his?" Hope rose in him.

"He's the CEO, for now. But now she has controlling stock." Star flopped down on the rattan sofa. "Have you ever met her?"

Adam shook his head, frowning. "Candice once mentioned that she had a wicked stepmother. She called her Genia. I didn't think anything else of it. Although," he said as he stroked his face, contemplating, "I wonder if she knows what's going on."

"What *is* going on, Adam?"

There wasn't much need to keep it a secret, given that Star knew so much already. He shoved his hands in his pockets. It was his turn to pace.

"Candice lied to her father, telling him I forced her to have an abortion. He pulled his business because of it. Now, if he buys out Thunder and the rest of my accounts jump ship because they think I'm unstable, then I'm out of business."

"Whoa." Star held up her hands. "Wait a minute. Why would she do that?"

He chuckled humorlessly, his voice flat. "She wants me to marry her. She'll lose her endowment, otherwise."

He felt as disgusted as the expression on Star's face.

"You've got to be kidding," she said, disbelieving.

"Wish I were," he said, sliding his hand over his head.

His thoughts flew to Mia, who he hoped was still in bed. As wonderful as it was being with her these last three days, he had to get back to work.

Lester Walker had just tightened the noose, and if he wanted to escape its grip he had to figure out a way to speed a decision out of Dorian Thibedeaux. A new idea was formulating in his head, too. Maybe talking to Eugenia Walker would be how he could save his company.

He spoke his thoughts. "I need to hear from Dorian Thibe—"

"Deaux?" Star cut in. "As in Dorian Thibedeaux, the hotel icon?" Star smiled slyly at him.

Adam felt a quickening in his stomach. He grasped her hand. "Please tell me you know this man from that mysterious job of yours."

"I know him. We had a hush-hush suicide attempt at one of his hotels not three months ago. I worked very closely with him to get this individual back to her home country without the press knowing anything about it."

"J.R. didn't mention it to me," Adam said.

Her expression closed. "That's because he didn't know, either. As far as the world is concerned, it never happened."

Adam saw her in a new light. Star was a heavy hitter. He got the sneaky feeling that she was involved with things they would never know about.

"I need to meet with Dorian again."

"I can do better than that." Star gathered her purse and briefcase, then linked arms with him, walking to the front door.

"He's invited to the wedding, and the reception is at his hotel."

"You're amazing," he said, kissing her cheek.

"I'm just glad you're not mad at me for being nosy. Really, I just wanted to help."

They stopped at the door, his hand on the knob. He could have been angry, but without her he wouldn't have the one option left of approaching Eugenia Walker with his business plan.

"I'm not angry," he said, hugging her. "If I pull this off, I'll owe you forever."

She hesitated. "The things we discussed . . ." she said, meeting his gaze squarely, "need to be kept confidential."

"I understand." Adam walked her outside and held the car door open for her.

"If Mia is feeling better, tell her to come over tonight. I need to pick out my invitations, have them printed tomorrow, and in the mail the day after tomorrow. I also have to decide on a dress."

"Mail them, and pick a dress, too? Are you waiting for something in particular, like a lightning strike?"

She laughed. "I have a friend who can print them, and another who can take care of the dress on short notice."

Adam nodded. Star had friends everywhere.

Mia listened to her messages. Star was the first, asking her to come over late that night.

She was pleasantly surprised at the next. "This is Charles. Your old friend from Chicago who hasn't heard from you in years." Mia smiled, massaging her forehead. Her fingers grazed the bandage, which sparked sensual memories of how she had spent the last three days.

Charles's voice snapped her back to the present.

"If you're not busy, call me at the Hotel Nikko. I would like to have dinner so we can discuss something very important."

She jotted down the number. The phone started to ring. Mia pressed the hold button on the answering machine, then picked up the phone. "Hello?"

"It's me, baby. Do you miss me yet?"

Mia smiled, the texture of his voice tickling her. "Mmm, I don't know. Who is this? I think you might have the wrong number."

His laughter triggered a warmth in her. "You have a mole at the top of your thigh. It's *delicious*. For an aerobics instructor you have remarkably smooth feet, although when your toes curled at *that* moment, I did think far off in the distance that you should cut your toenails."

Laughter bubbled from her.

"Shall I go on?" he said smoothly.

"No, I know you."

"How about dinner?"

Mia made regretful noises. "I can't. I have a dinner appointment with an old friend. Then I'm going over to Star's place to help her with wedding invitations and choose a bridal gown."

"Anybody I know?"

"No," she said evasively. Adam might not understand her relationship with Charles. He was from her previous life, someone that was connected to old memories.

"Anybody to worry about?" he said quietly.

"Not at all," she said. "I'll call you later. I'm probably going to spend the night at Star's place. We'll probably make it a late night."

"I'll probably hang out with J.R. Don't overdo it," he warned before they hung up.

Chapter 18

"I'm glad you could make it. You're looking quite well."

Mia sat across from her old colleague Charles Hawkins, and reminders of the past assaulted her. He had made the tough years at Loyola bearable. He was an intelligent and gifted doctor who took healing seriously, demanding as much from his students.

He taught them that half the battle was in believing. If you believed, and the patient believed, they had that much more of a chance of surviving the rigors of surgery than if they didn't.

Mia glanced around. Morgan's was still beautiful, but it had lost some of its allure, because she wasn't sitting across from Adam.

"Mia, we need you. Medicine needs you. You need to come home and join my practice."

She shook her head. "I don't know if I'm ready yet. I have a life here." Her thoughts shifted back to Adam and the three glorious days they spent together. Her skin pimpled and she brushed her arms. "I haven't practiced in two years. All I've done is keep up with my CME courses. I'm rusty. But—" she said as he cut her off.

"Mia, when you came into my office thirteen years ago you

asked me to take a chance on you, right?'' Ever the professional, he glanced around, lowering his voice discreetly.

"If I recall correctly, you said you would be dedicated until you die. You asked for my help and I gave it. Now I'm asking for yours. Do you remember the oath you swore?'' Charles pushed his spectacles down, where they teetered on the end of his pudgy nose. His bulging eyes remained fixed on her.

"I remember,'' she retorted, her temper rising. "But I also know I'm no good to anybody if I can't step into a hospital. I have to be able to be professional when I have to give parents bad news.'' Her voice shook, then leveled.

"I have to be able to keep my cool in an emergency, not lose it. There comes a point in a life threatening situation when you have to react on instincts. They failed me once when I needed them. I can't allow that to happen again.''

Mia's anger evaporated. "Right now, I'm not sure I'm ready.''

"It's not a volleyball game, Mia. You have to get right back in it. What you went through with Nikki can't stop you. I can only hold the position for you for one month.''

She eyed him speculatively when he extended his hand.

"Do we have a date?''

Mia shook his hand. "I can't promise that I'll move back to Chicago. But I'll have an answer for you one way or another.''

"Deal,'' he said. "That's good enough for me.''

Mia enjoyed the rest of the evening as Charles caught her up on local news and hospital gossip. Their conversation petered off as the waiter removed their plates and left the bill. He seemed more thoughtful, but she grew anxious to leave. She wanted to be somewhere else, with someone else.

He walked her to her car and she climbed in.

"You look very nice. You've been taking good care of yourself,'' he said, admiration coloring his tone.

Mia slid behind the wheel, and was surprised to see a look of longing on his face. It occurred to her that her medical abilities might not be the only reason Charles wanted her to return to Chicago.

"And this is a very nice car," he said, rubbing the top of the gold Lexus.

"It's not ... thanks." Mia cut off her explanation. She didn't owe Charles anything. Her feelings for him were strictly professional. She started the car and put it in reverse. Only then did she notice his hand still on the door.

"Are you all right, Doctor Hawkins?" Her tone snapped him out of his thoughts.

He looked at his hand, then removed it from the car, a small smile on his lips. "I'm fine." He seemed about to say something, then changed his mind.

"Goodnight, Mia."

She waved as she drove away.

"Isn't that Mia over there?" J.R. indicated the car at the end of the parking lot. Adam's hand was on the door handle of Morgan's, and he turned to look where J.R. was pointing.

His chest tightened when he saw the man leaning in the window of the Lexus, with Mia smiling up at him.

"I thought she was supposed to be at Star's tonight?" J.R. said.

Adam tried to shrug off the coincidence. "She said she had an appointment for tonight. She didn't say who with."

Jealousy burned within him, as the man seemed suddenly too chummy with her. Was he being a fool for her? Adam couldn't imagine Mia playing games with him, but lately, anything was possible. Candice's antics proved that. They only seemed to cause trouble in his life.

A little voice reminded him that Mia wasn't devious or conniving. He tried to reason with himself. There was probably a perfectly good explanation for her being there with another man.

"You want to just get our food to go and go back to your place and chill?" J.R. asked

"No," Adam said decisively. "I feel like crashing a pajama party."

"Hey girl, get in here." Star greeted her from the steps outside her condominium.

Mia hurried up and gave her friend a quick hug.

The few times she had been to Star's house had been an adventure. Hardwood floors throughout, it had a sophisticated air that was pure Star. Her taste was expensive, and it showed in the sculptures and art that covered the tables and walls.

"How are you feeling?" Star asked, peering at her intently.

"Good, I feel fine," she said as she followed her to the kitchen.

Star's lips curved. "Just fine? Not great?"

"Okay, you nosy pervert. I hope you feel better since you know." she said, a silly grin on her face.

"I sure do." Star clapped, laughing.

Mia stared at the dining room table. "Who is going to go through all this?" she demanded when Star brought in three boxes of invitations, place cards, bridal magazines, and other assorted samples.

Adopting her best Southern accent, Star drawled, "Why, we are. Would you like sweet tea, or something stronger?"

"If we're doing this all night, then I'd better stick with the nonalcoholic beverages. I can't believe you're planning to get married next weekend. Nobody will be able to come at this late notice."

"All fifty of our relatives already know. We're just mailing these as keepsakes."

They separated all the items into categories and got down to business. Glancing over at her friend, Mia looked at her closely. It was obvious that she was in love. Her green eyes glowed every time she mentioned J.R.'s name, or when she thought he would like something she picked out. "Star?"

"Hmm?"

"When did you know you were in love?"

Star placed some green invitations in the trash pile and folded her hands in front of her. "I've been attracted to J.R. for a long time. We started dating over a year ago, but neither of us wanted to get serious. I guess we got comfortable with the relationship we had. He had a mother who walked out on him, and my parents died when I was very young. But it was after Grace's funeral that we knew we loved each other enough to make this big commitment.

"Something changed us there. Maybe it was being able to grieve together. Or maybe it was standing next to Adam, who was truly alone at that cemetery. Without us, there was no family there for him."

"How sad," Mia said, her heart going out to him.

"But I just know that after it was over I knew I couldn't live without him. He's my best friend." Her voice softened. "And he's an excellent lover. And I love everything there is about him."

Mia continued to sift through the invitations, eliminating those that weren't textured.

"Since this is girl talk," Star said, "I want to ask you something. What are you waiting for? Adam is so right for you. You guys have—" she searched for the word, her hands expressively flying through the air. "Chemistry. What's holding you back?"

Mia could only shrug. She couldn't explain that she didn't want any more children who would die on her. Adam wanted a family, and that was the one thing she couldn't give him.

She shrugged again. "It's hard for me to talk about it. I just hope we won't get to the phase you're in for a long, long time."

"You're thinking of it all wrong. You love him." Star held

up her hands to stop Mia's argument. "Once you face it, taking the next step will be easy."

Mia wished she could believe it.

She yanked on a gold corner until a sparkling invitation was in her hand. "What do you think of this one?"

Star *aah'd* and took it from her fingers. "I love it!" Mia wasn't at all surprised when she put it in the "potential" pile.

"Did you hear something?" Star held the wine bottle over her glass, draining the rest into her glass.

Mia sat up, listening intently. "I didn't hear a thing," she whispered. "Go see."

Star left, then ran back.

"There's somebody at the door."

Mia stood abruptly. "Call the police," she whispered.

"I'm going to see." Star grabbed the empty bottle and brandished it, going into the hall. Mia followed with the broom.

Star threw open the front door.

"Hah!"

"Hah!" J.R. and Adam yelled back.

Mia looked suspiciously at them. "You set me up," she said to Star, who smiled victoriously.

"I wish I *had* set this up. I'm just as surprised as you to see these handsome guys at my door. Come on, honey, let's go upstairs," she said to J.R. She winked at them as they disappeared up the stairs.

"You're dangerous," Adam said, taking the broom from her hand and putting it in the hall closet. He wrapped his arm around her waist.

"Aren't you going to kiss me hello?" Mia said, looking at him through lowered lids.

"Most definitely." His lips covered hers possessively. Mia opened, allowing his tongue to probe into the feathery depths of her mouth, loving the taste of him. The yearning built in her again. Even after spending three wonderful days with him, she hadn't had enough.

"Hello, Mia," he murmured against her lips.

"Hello, Adam."

They linked hands on the way to the den. Adam led her to a love seat big enough for two. Adam's posture was stiff, even after his toe curling kiss.

"Hey, what's up?"

"If I ask you a direct question, will you give me a straight answer?"

"Yes." Mia licked her lips and folded her hands together to keep from fidgeting.

A stray curl had fallen from her loose knot and she tucked it behind her ear, pulled it out, then tucked it in again. All this time Adam watched closely, a serious expression covering his face.

She couldn't bear his scrutiny any longer. "Adam—"

"This evening," he began, "I went to Morgan's for dinner with J.R. I saw you there with another man, and I want to know if you're involved with him."

"No." She sighed, relieved. "That was Doctor Charles Hawkins. He's my mentor from medical school. I'm not involved with him in any way other than as friends. He popped into town and we had dinner." Mia omitted an important part of their dinner discussion. But she wasn't ready to think about returning to medicine or Chicago.

She shifted her position on the chair, making room for his long legs.

"You looked as if you were enjoying yourself. Is there anything else? Maybe something about him and you I should know? I like to know the enemy," he said, stroking his finger down her arm. "It makes it easier to win the battle."

"Battle?" Mia barely eked the word past the dryness of her lips. Her tongue darted out to moisten them.

"Yes, the battle," he said, tipping her chin towards him. "I'm in love with you, Mia Jacobs."

"Oh, my God, don't say that."

Adam pulled her up to face him. "Don't tell me how to feel

or what to say. I love you, and that's that.'' He stole her breath
away with his devouring kiss.

Mia returned it with the love she carried in her heart for
him.

''We're good together,'' he said when they separated. ''Don't
forget it. I'll be right back,'' he said, and left her alone.

Mia rested her hand on her head, feeling the Band-Aid that
covered the gash. It had scabbed over and was shrinking each
day. It hardly even hurt anymore. She stroked it gingerly, thinking of how Adam cared for her. Loved her.

She closed her eyes, dreaming of him with their children,
taking them to the gardens and patiently teaching them everything he knew about flowers and plants. She snuggled her head
into her arm, seeing herself pregnant and his loving reaction
to it. It was glorious and wonderful.

Mia dreamed, allowing the warmth and security of his love
surpass the fear that was always with her.

It was all right, she dreamed. When he returned and snuggled
against her, that felt all right, too.

Adam's fingers flew across the computer keys as he absorbed
the information with lightning speed. The numbers were still
the same. By the end of the month, he would have to lay off
at least ten people, before the end of the year, everyone, if
business didn't turn around.

He had won the Thunder account, but only by offering
unprecedented discounts, with his company gaining more profit
percentage over the next two years.

The Thunder account team hadn't wanted to commit the
remaining stores, but he had negotiated them in.

There were families counting on him.

The phone buzzed, and he wondered who would be calling
him at five in the morning. *Mia.* He pushed the button, expecting
to hear her voice.

''Hey, baby. Do you miss me?''

"Adam? It's me, Candice. I'm giving a dinner party tonight because I need to show Eugenia that I'm close to getting married. I need you to escort me."

Adam snatched the receiver. "Have you lost your mind?" he ground out. "As far as I'm concerned, you don't exist."

"Adam, I really need your help." Her voice grew shaky. "What can somebody like me do? I don't have any skills to speak of—"

"I don't care. You'll land on your feet. You always do." An idea occurred to him. "Your stepmother is in town tonight?"

Instantly her voice brightened. He cringed. She wasn't even a good actress. "She's having dinner at my father's house tonight. You can pick me up at five. We'll have cocktails—"

Adam hung up the phone, a plan formulating in his head.

Chapter 19

Adam uncurled his long frame from his car in front of Lester Walker's stucco colonial home. It was four-thirty in the afternoon. He had called for an appointment at the last minute and was told to be there within the hour.

He hoped he had guessed right, that Lester and Candice wouldn't be there. It was imperative that he be given the opportunity to make his proposal without their lies clouding the issue of his business.

Adam grabbed the bouquet of flowers from the front seat of the car and debated whether he should take them. He nixed the idea. He wouldn't bring flowers to a man.

Briefcase, straighten tie, smile. Adam checked himself, then rang the doorbell. The strains of Beethoven's Fifth Symphony played before the door was answered by a middle-aged woman.

"Eugenia Walker, please," he said, extending his business card. "Tell her Adam Webster is calling."

She ushered him into the sitting room, where he sat on a beige brocade couch. He declined her offer of coffee and rested his briefcase by his feet. Adam tried to quell his nervousness, but the weight of today's decision rested on his shoulders.

Looking around, he could see why he had always disliked

this house. It was cold and impersonal, with no reminders of family around. It had a cheerless atmosphere that was isolating.

Adam rose and walked to the window, inserting his hand in his pocket. The layered drapes obscured his view, and he forced himself to be calm. He wanted this business, but he wouldn't beg.

"Mr. Webster?"

He turned quickly. "Yes."

"Mrs. Walker will see you now."

Adam strode behind the woman, who handed him his briefcase at the door of the library with an assuring smile.

He thanked her when she reached up and straightened his tie, with a wink. She mouthed *good luck,* and he walked inside.

Eugenia Walker stood tall and regal at a Queen Anne desk. Stylishly dressed, she rounded it, extending a delicate hand to him. He took it and was surprised at its strength.

"Mr. Webster, so good of you to come. Would you care for something to drink before you explain why I shouldn't back my husband's decision to cease all business with your company?"

"No, thank you," Adam said, smiling politely. Inside, he felt his stomach drop. "You would be doing your company a great disservice if you based your decision on a personal disagreement, Mrs. Walker. My products are top quality from the best producers in the world. We can handle the volume your stores demand. Webster's reputation is outstanding."

It took her a moment before she motioned for him to follow her to a round conference table.

He spread out his proposal, presenting her with a copy, and for the next forty minutes presented his company's business plan. They bantered about pricing and disagreed on delivery dates for holiday products, eventually compromising.

At the end of the hour, Adam snapped his briefcase closed. "Do we have a deal?"

Eugenia Walker smiled, crossing her legs, tapping the eraser of her pencil on the table.

"Yes, we do." She nodded.

Adam shook her extended hand, jubilation coursing through him. To say he was surprised by Eugenia Walker would have been a gross understatement. He was bowled over by her knowledge, professionalism, and the fact that she had single-handedly put his company back on its feet.

"May I ask you a question?" Adam said.

"I see." Her southern accent was lilting. "Now that we have a deal, you want to sneak something else in." She *tsked*.

"Not at all," he said, comfortable. "I was curious about why you would want to work with me, after what you've heard about me from your family."

"Blood is thicker than water, Mr. Webster. That's true. But business is business. I wasn't sure about anything until you showed up today. You had nothing to lose by coming here today. I also appreciated the fact that you didn't come here to disparage my stepdaughter or husband, but to work. I respect that," she continued.

"You're a sharp young man, who's running a successful business. And," she added with a sly smile. "You give great discounts. Too bad my stepdaughter couldn't appreciate you for who you truly are." She rose and extended her hand to him. "Have your attorneys draw up the contracts and send them to me."

Adam squeezed her hand appreciatively. "Thank you," he said as she walked him back to the front door.

"No, thank *you*. Have a good day, Adam."

Adam stood outside the house, feeling as if it were Christmas.

The dashboard clock reflected the time as he drove back toward the office. He exited the next ramp, to downtown traffic at a dead standstill. The back roads had faster moving traffic, and he took them, knowing nobody was leaving until he returned. This meeting was too important.

He entered the conference room that held all his employees.

They were lined against the walls, and a hush settled over the room when he walked in.

Adam prolonged the moment by loosening his tie and taking great pains to place his briefcase perfectly on the table. Everyone leaned forward when he opened his mouth.

"We got the business."

Excitement charge the air. Teresa, his cool account executive, started crying, while others whooped, laughing and clapping.

Angela ordered pizza and soda, turning their celebration into an office party. Adam accepted their praise, shaking hands and personally thanking each one of them.

"Sir, the phone is for you," Angela said, tugging on his sleeve.

He picked up the line in the conference room. Sticking his finger in his ear, he asked incredulously, "How much?"

Adam thought because of the noise of the party he had heard the total wrong.

"Fifteen hundred dollars!" he yelled. "What are you doing? Rebuilding Mia's car from the body in?" Adam started laughing. "The door fell off. Yeah, fix it."

He grabbed his jacket. He wanted to see his baby.

Mia marched behind her step, looking into the mirror at the class behind her. "Lunge, after five, four, three, two, one."

The class changed steps and lunged off the back of the platforms, thrusting their arms in the air.

She kept a watchful eye on them as she demonstrated the same routine from the stage. She reached out without breaking stride and flicked the switch for the fans, circulating cool air. Appreciative whistles from some of the members let her know they were thankful.

"You okay, Scout?" she asked, turning around on the step to watch him. He gave her the thumbs up.

"In five, go to basic, then knee up straddle, corner to corner, then everybody's favorite, around the world."

Mia turned her back to the class and gave the countdown. "Five, four, three, two." Out of the corner of her eye she caught Scout's misstep.

"One," she said.

It seemed to happen in slow motion. Scout leaned over, and his body went crashing to the floor.

Mia jumped off the stage, throwing her headset to the floor, racing to his side. Pandemonium broke loose, with people scattering everywhere. She kneeled beside him, trying to free his limp body from Helen, who screamed, grabbing her husband's waist.

"Scout, answer me," she said around Helen's crying. "Can you hear me?" she asked louder, and received no response.

Helen screamed again. Mia scanned the room, looking for someone who could hold back the hysterical woman. Two male members of the class stepped up, guiding her a short distance away from him.

"Call an ambulance," she said, and motioned another man forward. "Help me turn him over."

Carefully they rolled his unconscious body until he lay on his back. Quickly she checked his carotid pulse. It beat unsteadily—then it was gone. Mia leaned over his face and detected no breathing.

"Back up," she ordered the onlookers who crowded around. She checked his mouth and placed his head back to clear his breathing passage. Her fingers deftly slid along Scout's sternum, finding the proper spot.

Lacing her fingers, she began the rhythmic compressions, setting a steady pace. She stopped to breathe into his mouth, then resumed the compressions. Mia counted aloud, then began the cycle again.

Five times she repeated the compressions and breathing, noticing no change in his condition. His eyes remained half closed, his mouth slack. She stopped to check his pulse.

There was none.

Distantly, she heard someone say the ambulance was on the

way and she nodded, her arms burning from the pressure of the constant pumping. Sweat dripped off her nose, and Mia brushed her face on her shoulder before breathing short puffs into his mouth, saying a silent prayer.

"Come on, Scout," she pleaded as she compressed again. "Breathe." *Live.*

He gurgled as she pressed his chest, then blinked, groaning hoarsely. Bile ran from his mouth and she turned his head to the side, relief flooding her.

Just then the paramedics arrived and assumed control of the situation, swiftly preparing him to be transported to the hospital. They rushed him into the ambulance, and Mia assisted Helen into her car.

The emergency room was only a few minutes from the club, and thankfully they arrived quickly. Scout was conscious, but in tremendous pain when they entered the short hallway, and he was quickly wheeled away from them into an emergency room.

"Helen, you have to try to stop crying," Mia said, her voice stern but compassionate. "You're not going to be able to help Scout if you're sick, too." She hugged the woman, who sagged into her shoulder, her body racked with sobs.

She sympathized with her, but when she started to hyperventilate Mia called in a physician who prescribed a mild sedative.

They were moved to a private waiting room out of the main area of the hospital. All six of the Cooperman's children arrived, in various stages of distress, and she tried to comfort them until Josh cornered her.

"Were you teaching the class when he," he swallowed with difficulty, "had the attack?"

"Yes," she said apologetically, noticing his glance over her clothes. "There wasn't time to change. I guess I should go," she said reluctantly.

Josh shook his head. "We want you to stay. You're the reason why we're here, and not planning his funeral. Thank you.'' His voice clogged with tears and his brother and sister embraced him, taking him to a nearby chair.

''Doctor Jacobs?''

''Yes,'' she said, turning.

''You might not remember me, but my name is Odessa Reuben, and my son is Nigel Reuben. Remember? His lip?''

Mia nodded. Her son had been born with a cleft lip, and she had had a hard time accepting his impairment.

''How is Nigel?'' Mia asked, remembering how lively the boy had become as he got older.

''He's quite a prankster, thanks to you,'' Odessa said, smiling. ''I brought you some clothes,'' she said, handing a nurses outfit to her. The pants were green and the top an array of splattered pastel colors. Mia slipped them on over her workout outfit.

''How are you?'' she asked, feeling better now that she was covered.

''I'm fine. Thanks to you.'' Her shy voice gained strength as she talked. ''I didn't think I could handle a child with a birth defect. I was always thinking about what other people would think of me. But I went to that counselor you recommended, and I'm a changed person.''

Odessa took her hands, squeezing, her eyes filled with tears, her voice humbled.

''You saved my family and I never got to thank you. I didn't think that was you when you first walked in, I mean you've lost weight and cut your hair, but then I thought, where else would she be? Helping somebody, of course.''

She hugged Mia quickly, leaving her speechless.

''I've got to go back to work, but if you have a private practice I would like to bring Nigel and his two little sisters to you.''

''Two little sisters?'' Mia said, awed.

''Twins.'' Odessa smiled tenderly. Love radiated from her. Mia stepped outside the private waiting room, with Odessa giving her one final hug.

"I'll call you, if I ever get one."

"Take care, Doctor," Odessa said, waving.

"You too," Mia said, suddenly enjoying the sound of her title.

Word of Scout's condition came late that afternoon. He would need another bypass operation, but he was stabilized for the night. Mia sat with his children for a while longer, then left the hospital, returning to the club.

She noticed how it was business as usual. The cheerful atmosphere felt strange, and she stuck her head in the weight room, looking around. "Anybody seen J.R.?"

The men grunted, and she took that as no.

"Adam was looking for you earlier," one commented, bench pressing four hundred pounds.

"Thanks," she said, ducking out. It was just as well that she had missed him, she thought as she headed to the staff dressing room. She wanted to be alone.

Mia stripped and stepped into the shower, letting the hot water soothe her. The drama began to unfold again for her, and she shivered.

"Mia!"

The steam from the shower clouded her view as she fumbled for her towel. "Right here," she sniffled, cutting off the water, covering herself.

"I was looking for you," Adam said, dragging her into his arms. She soaked his suit down the front and tried to push away, but the strength she garnered from his touch melted her remaining control.

She sniffed and shook, then stood still. "You're all wet," she said into his neck. "Somebody might come in here."

"I don't care. I heard about it earlier and I couldn't find you. Somebody told me you went to the hospital."

He peered at her. "Are you okay?"

Her heartbeat quickened, her body responding instantly to him. She nodded and stepped away, going to her locker.

Mia wiped her face with the corner of the towel and squared

her shoulders. "I'm going to be fine," she said, her voice shaking.

Adam turned her and slid his hands up her arms, bringing her to him. He held her to him, and rocked her.

It wasn't planned, the tender way he reassured her or how the holes in her heart seemed to heal. But all her doubt slipped away as if it never existed.

"Mmm," he groaned, chuckling. "I can't be this close to you without thinking of us together, forever."

Mia stepped back, feeling like a trapdoor had closed.

"I'd better get dressed before we get in trouble," she said, avoiding the subject of forever.

Instead, she pulled the towel tighter around her. Adam noticed her shaking hands and tilted her chin up.

"I'll be outside. Are you up for the wedding rehearsal tonight?"

"Give me half an hour," she said, and took her battling thoughts into the next room to get dressed.

Was it just his imagination, or was Mia avoiding him?

Adam thought back over the last two weeks and counted the number of times they had been together. It hadn't been more than twice. Those were because of the rehearsals for the wedding. Even their conversations over the phone were stilted and hurried. Something had changed.

Ever since that evening when she had dinner with her college mentor, as she called him, she had grown distant.

Adam tried to control his jealous feelings. He had even backed off because of her ordeal with the old man at the club.

"Dammit," he swore, dropping the bow tie again.

What if she just doesn't love me? Finally the tie clipped on his shirt. He checked the tails on his tuxedo and picked up the velvet box that contained Star's wedding ring.

Adam glanced at the shimmery baguette diamonds and hoped one day it would be him and Mia.

He snapped the box closed. The sound reverberated against the walls in the hotel bathroom and helped him to come to a conclusion.

This weekend would make the difference. One way or another he would find out where they stood.

Chapter 20

The wedding was anything but typical as Adam waited to see her. He hadn't seen her dress, but he imagined what she would look like in it. The magazine picture Star showed him earlier that week wasn't enough.

Ociano roses adorned each row, with an intricate bouquet woven into an eight-foot arching trellis, where the wedding party and minister would stand.

Jazzed up chords of wedding music quieted the crowd, and the lights dimmed. The room was bathed in soft candlelight. Shadows cast over the crowd of fifty guests, and everyone's head turned toward the door.

Set off by the firelight, Mia was a vision of loveliness as the gold dress she wore sparkled against the flickering orange flames. Adam gasped, as did most of the crowd. She was absolutely stunning.

She glided toward him, the gold sleek dress prolonging her approach. It curved and hugged her in all the right places, and he couldn't take his eyes off her.

Her hair was pinned high, leaving her neck free. Adorned with bold, gold earrings, she was a beautiful princess.

Adam tried to stop undressing her with his eyes, but when

they stood beside each other it was all he could do not to take her in his arms and make her confess her undying love for him.

He lost the chance once the music began for Star's approach. She, too, was stunning, in a cream, formfitting dress that flared at the bottom around her ankles. One shoulder was bare, and in her hand she carried a russet, cream, and pink rose bouquet that almost touched the floor.

Adam was unaccustomed to J.R.'s seriousness, but he understood how much this meant to him. The ceremony was over in twenty minutes. Everyone cheered when J.R. kissed Star until tears ran from her eyes.

Adam helped usher the guests into the next room, where the reception was being held. The decor was unforgettable, and Adam fought his jealousy. He wanted to be him.

Half the night passed before Mia came to talk with him.

"Having a good time?" she asked, her eyes scanning the crowd. *Who was she looking for?*

"Yeah," he replied. "Waiting for somebody?" he asked, tilting her chin up.

"You." She smiled seductively. "To ask me to stay the night with you."

He brushed aside the interrupting hand that exerted pressure on his arm. "You ask me," he said, releasing her.

"Adam, can I," she whispered, glancing over his shoulder, "can I stay with you tonight?"

He nodded, a slow grin spreading over his face.

"Blow me a kiss when you're ready." He watched her glide away.

Star chose that moment to interrupt. "Adam, you've met Dorian. He's an old friend who will take good care of you," she said, and was off.

"It's good to see you, Dorian. I don't take favors," Adam said, establishing the ground rules.

"I don't do them," Dorian said, sipping champagne. "I like a man who stands on his own two feet."

"And I like a man who has the answer I want to hear. What's your decision?" Adam volleyed back.

Dorian extended his hand. "Your ideas are revolutionary. They'll take us into the twenty-first century, and probably beyond. I can have the contracts delivered to your attorney's office tomorrow. Barring any unforeseen circumstances, do we have a deal?"

Adam's eyes lingered on the outstretched hand. His life had just turned another corner, in a matter of a few weeks. It was more than he could ever dream of. Now there was only one piece that eluded him.

"We have a deal," he said, and shook.

The music lowered and Pops called for the toast to the bride and groom from the best man.

Adam hurried to the microphone and laced fingers with Mia, who had come to stand beside him. Mia looked at him adoringly. His heart burst.

Adam hardly remembered what he said, but it must have been good, because people cheered when he set the microphone on the banquet table. They cheered more when the four friends hugged. The band started to play and Adam turned to Mia.

"Are we leaving?" He met her gaze and saw the flicker of desire in them.

She kissed his cheek. "I'm ready."

The ride to his suite was swift.

Mia started pulling pins from her hair, and he strained to keep from undressing her in the hallway.

They stepped inside and she gasped in surprise.

Rose petals were sprinkled all over the floor, making a floral path. The hairpins slid from her hand as she took his hand and walked into the bedroom.

Adam started to remove his tie, but she stopped him, taking it off herself, following it with his jacket and shirt.

She placed her hands on his chest and kissed it, sliding them

up until they wound around his neck. He ignited a fire in her
that she had suppressed too long.

Mia molded herself to him, the thin silk dress no match for
the hard planes of his body. Her nipples jutted against the
fabric, responding to his nearness.

He trailed his mouth down her throat, dragging the long
zipper down her back. Mia stepped out of the dress and stood
before him in just thin wisps of lace. She reached back and
unsnapped her bra. It eased forward off her arms as she moved,
and he swallowed, watching the seductive strip.

Before she reached him her mouth opened ready to accept
his plundering tongue. The wiry hairs on his chest tickled her
breasts until they hardened, almost painfully. Mia leaned back,
ecstasy growing when he covered the brown top with his mouth.

He sucked hungrily, as if life's sustenance flowed from them.
Adam lifted her around her waist and carried her to the rose
petal-covered bed. He unfastened the black tuxedo pants, which
fell to the floor unaided. His arousal pushed against the silk
boxer shorts which dropped as well, followed quickly to the
floor by his socks.

Mia's triangular panties and thigh-high stockings proved no
barrier to his desire to have her naked. They were quickly
discarded. He lowered himself beside her.

His probing kisses and masterful hands left her quivering by
the time he reached her toes.

Adam worked his way back up to her breasts, where he
stayed until her cries of ecstasy bounced off the walls. She
pleaded with him to end the sweet torture, yet he slowed them
down, taking his time, making her wait.

"You're gorgeous," he said in her ear, his hands sliding
down her hot skin, possessively grabbing hold of her bottom.
He rolled her on top of him and she pressed, until he growled
deep in his throat.

"I can't wait,"

"Don't," she gasped, snatching the condom from the night
table. Her fingers shook as he continued to inch lower until he

was just below her opening. She had never been so desired before, and it took all her control not to just settle on him and end it. The rubber slid into her hands, and she kissed his tip before sheathing him.

His cries to all the saints made every fiber of her yearn for him, and she moaned when he parted her.

How he slowed her down, easing her away from the climax that threatened, she would never know, but the urgency she felt cooled, making their lovemaking tender and sensual.

He slipped from her, laying her back against the silky sheets, then slid into her again, resuming their pace.

"You feel good," he murmured, nipping her neck. The hardness of his thrust and the soft love bites made her squirm in deep pleasure.

She slanted her lips under his, taking his tongue deep in her mouth, her hands grabbing his butt, making him push harder. A fire started in the soles of her feet, spreading until it consumed every muscle in her body, and she clenched, quivering, spinning.

"More," she gasped.

The whispered plea made him laugh a sharp, breathless sound which she found thrilling, especially since he had pleased her so much already.

"Greedy," he replied, and gave her what she asked for.

Whispered words filled her ears and he told her everywhere he would suck her, lick and taste her.

With the swift motions of his hips, the erotic, carnal words and his hand between her, stimulating her womanly nub, Mia screeched over passion's cliff, shattering into brilliant, splendid shock waves of satisfaction.

They stayed locked in each other's embrace until the cool air in the room made goose bumps jump out on her skin.

Adam moved first, causing her to gasp when he slid from her, leaving his latex protector.

She squirmed, laughing when he fished for it, before tossing it in the trash.

"Did I hurt you?" He asked, his hand still caressing her. "No," she said, her voice already thick with desire.

Adam took his hand from her.

"I can't think of a better time to say this." Adam sat up in the bed, his muscles rippling as he reached for his shorts.

From the expression on his face, she could tell he had something important on his mind. Her leg jumped, and her eye twitched.

He looked at her and his eyes confirmed his words.

"I love you. I've loved you since the first day I saw you in that cemetery, wet and crying. I want us to be together." His voice softened. "I want to marry you. I want us to build a life and family together."

Mia raised slowly. She was speechless. He was the man she loved with all her heart, but there was something holding her back. Her throat closed around the words she wanted to say. *I love you,* echoed in her head.

Instead she said, "I need some time."

To her surprise he sighed, a look of relief on his face. "I thought you were going to say no."

"I can't just say no to you." She kneeled in front of him and wiggled her fingers. He came to her. Mia planted soft kisses on his chest. Her lips softly touched his breasts. "I won't take long."

"Good. I want you in my life forever. It's not a now or never situation. I can wait a couple of days."

"Let's go back to bed," she suggested, glad he wasn't pressuring her.

His body responded for her.

"What time is checkout?" Mia called from the bathroom while Adam checked his messages.

It had been a blissful two days, and she wouldn't tell Adam, but she was sore in the best way she'd ever been.

Mia zipped up the gold silk dress and pulled her hair back

in a severe ponytail. That was the best she could do, given that
she hadn't planned to stay away from home overnight.

"It's twelve o'clock," he said from the doorway.

He was so handsome with the collar of his shirt open at the
neck and a light beard covering his face. His dark eyes swung
over her appreciatively, and she felt that old familiar rush.

"Don't look at me like that. We *have* to leave. The hotel is
going to charge us for an extra day."

Mia tipped her head to the side and pierced her ear with her
earring.

"A golden princess," he murmured from behind her, ignoring her warning. He pulled her down on his lap as he sat on
the edge of the Jacuzzi tub.

"This feels familiar," he said seductively, and she spun with
deliberate slowness, purposely grinding herself into him.

"Yeah, it is," she said, kissing his full lips.

Sex wasn't meant to be so good, she had thought often that
weekend. Adam wasn't afraid of anything, and even when she
thought her body wouldn't cooperate, he showed her how it
could be done. Frankly, she was surprised that so many people
made it to work every day.

"I have a surprise for you," he said, cupping her breast
through her dress.

"Mmm," she groaned when his finger teased her nipple.
"What?"

"Your car is ready."

"Mmm—What?" She took her lips from him to look into
his eyes.

He nodded, a crease of amusement around his mouth.

"They delivered it to your house yesterday."

"I don't believe it," she said, embarrassed. "I forgot all
about it."

"Not too hard to do in that Lexus," he said, his hands
spanning her waist. He urged her up. "I need to stop at work,
but I thought we could meet later."

"Sure, what time?" she asked, following him from the bathroom.

"How about seven?"

"Seven's good," she said, getting one final kiss before he locked the suite behind them.

Chapter 21

Mia shoved on the door again, loosening it from the door-jamb. She jiggled the key out of the lock and walked into her apartment, waving her hand under her nose.

The two-day old air was stale and smelled of smoke. The ventilation system was probably older than the building, she thought smartly, or the neighbors enjoyed burnt food.

It's time to move, she thought as she kneeled on the couch to raise the window. *Time to make some decisions.*

Adam's proposal whipped through her mind. It warmed her and frightened her at the same time. He had certainly given her enough cause to say yes. *And I did, several times,* she thought, blushing.

But a family.

Her heart hammered at the thought of being pregnant. Of morning sickness, and the fluttering movement of a baby inside her. But holding the little wonder in her arms, kissing it, loving it, made the fear less important, minute.

Mia walked around the studio apartment looking at the life she created for herself two years ago. It had been fine, then. A place to heal and rebuild. But now, two years later, it was stifling in its closeness.

She reached around and unzipped her dress, shrugging it off her shoulders, throwing it on the bed. She turned and noticed the answering machine's steady blinks. Lying across the bed, she pressed *Play*.

Mia wasn't surprised at the first.

"It's Charles Hawkins. I believe we talked one month ago tomorrow. I need your decision by nine in the morning. Thank you," he added as an afterthought and hung up.

Mia rolled her eyes. He was much too formal. For Pete's sake, he had been closer to her than most men. He delivered Nikki.

She dragged the dress off the bed and walked to the closet. The padded hanger it had come off days ago was empty, and she hung it up with the other clothes that needed to go to the cleaners. Her short purple robe hung on the door, and she picked it up.

The machine beeped.

"Mia, it's Mom." Her mother's tearful voice filled the room. Mia dropped the robe and rushed to the bed. Fear tore through her, and she felt faint.

"Honey, you need to come home. We have some terrible, horrible news," she sobbed. Then her father's voice came on brokenly.

"The bastard confessed. The D.A. let him make a deal. You have to come home—" The machine cut them off and rewound itself.

The pain of losing Nikki came back, and she screamed and screamed until her throat was raw. Mia wished she had been run over by a truck. She didn't want to feel that tortuous pain again. It ripped into her like a knife, and she doubled over, falling to her knees, it hurt so much.

She could make out voices at her door, concerned voices that wondered what was happening. She just couldn't move to tell them to get help.

Because there was none.

There were no pills or medicine that could fix where she

hurt. The phone rang, and she lay paralyzed by her anguish. "Baby, it's me. I hope you're still coming over tonight." His deep voice held a note of promise. "I just wanted you to know that I love you." He paused. "I wish you were there so I could tell you I love you. That's it."

He hung up as she raised from the floor. She had to see him.

Chapter 22

Adam hung up the phone as the doorbell chimed. He opened it, then stopped short.

"Candice. What do you want?"

She walked in uninvited and made herself comfortable in the den. Adam pushed the front door.

"Planning for company?" she asked, picking up a kernel of popcorn, popping it into her mouth. She inspected an empty wineglass, then replaced it on the table.

"That's none of your business," he said, his voice edged, growing angrier. "You have ten seconds to say why you're here and then you're out." He checked his watch.

"Start talking. Ten," he said impatiently. "Nine, eight, seven."

"Reconsider," she said, coming toward him.

"No. Six, five, four."

"I need you to do this for me. Eugenia is divorcing my father. What will happen to me?"

He shrugged. "Get a job. Three, two, one. Time's up. Goodbye, Candice."

The front door slammed open.

"Adam." The way Mia wailed his name was like fingernails

Carmen Green

on a chalkboard. Adam turned toward the door as she approached, and Candice took his hesitation as her opportunity to launch herself at him. Her lips pressed against his as Mia rounded the corner of the den.

Her mouth sprang open. Her eyes were bloodshot from crying, and she looked as if she were traumatized.

Candice smiled victoriously. Mia turned and ran back through the front door.

"Get out!" Adam ground out as he shoved past her.

When he got to the driveway, Mia was struggling with the new door on her car, trying to open it.

"That wasn't what you think," he offered by way of explanation.

"Nothing ever is," she said through hiccups. He touched her arm to stop her frantic pulling.

"Baby, you know that I love you and that I would never do anything to hurt you." He didn't understand her pain, and tried to wipe at the tears that streamed from her eyes.

She cringed. "I can't marry you."

"What?" he said, his voice just above a whisper.

"I'm accepting a job in Chicago. I—I just—" she stumbled over her words. "I just came by to tell you I was leaving."

"Nothing," she said evasively, her hands shaking like spring leaves.

"Then why are you running? I'm here. I love you. And you love me," he said, trying to control his growing anger. He was tired of fighting. Tired of trying to convince her of his love. Tired of being alone.

He wanted to shake someone, to yell, to shout at the top of his lungs. For once he wanted to lose control.

She was breaking his heart and didn't care. He took her by the arm. "Let's go in the house and talk."

"No," she said, garnering enough strength to pull away. "I can't. I'm driving home tonight. I have to—" She wiped hair out of her eyes. "I have to go."

Candice walked out on the steps and made a pooh-pooh sound. Adam lost it. He pointed at her, his voice low and deadly. "Get off my property, before—" He struggled, wanting to wrap his hands around her neck and squeeze. "Before I use you as fertilizer in my yard."

Candice hurried to her car and burned rubber off his driveway. Adam turned back to Mia, who had finally gotten the key into the car lock.

"Is this how you resolve all your problems?" he yelled. "To run and shut out everybody who loves you?" He jabbed his finger into the hood of the car. "Ever since I met you you've been doing the same thing. Running. From me. From yourself. When are you going to stop?"

She didn't answer.

"I lost somebody, too. No, it wasn't my daughter, but I loved her just the same. But you know what? She wanted me to keep on living, to find happiness." He drew an exasperated breath. "I found you."

"I can't give you what you want, Adam. I can't give you a family." The car door creaked open.

He shook his head, defeated. His heart cried out, but he kept it in, fighting the emotion. He could chase her to the ends of the earth and back, but if she didn't want him it wouldn't matter what he did.

"Go ahead and go," he said, throwing up his hands. "I'm not going to stop you. You seem to find your best answers on your own."

Adam stepped back from the car as Mia slid into the seat. He dropped his hands to his hips and watched her drive away, a tear dropping off her chin as she went.

Chapter 23

Mia sat on the front steps of the place she had called home for many years, and let the Indian summer breeze drift over her. The screen door slapped shut behind her and she turned her head, waiting for her father's familiar shuffle to scrape on the wooden porch.

"Catching a cool breeze?" he said, pleasantly. "It's a rare day in October when it gets this warm. Your Mama's gone to the mall. We won't see her until late tonight."

Mia scooted over as he favored his good leg to sit beside her. He huffed when his rotund body finally landed on the top step. She absently rubbed his back, staring into the distance.

"You used to do that when you were a little girl," he said wistfully.

The corners of her lips turned up, and she continued the rhythmic motion. They sat quietly, the companionable silence growing between them. She rested her chin on her other arm, and closed her eyes when the breeze lifted her hair and flapped it on her shoulders.

"Mia, I owe you an apology."

She stopped rubbing to look at him. "For what?"

"For not loving you the way a good father should have."

"That's not true," she blurted, but stopped when he held
up his hand.

"Don't try to change my apology. I know what I did," he
said gruffly. "I should have let you cry when you were a child.
I should have let you speak your piece when you were young."
His gaze dropped to his hands. "Maybe you wouldn't be so
quiet now, and cry all by yourself."

"Daddy." Her voice broke and she threw her arms around
her father. Mia's body shook as he rocked her, making up for
lost years.

"I'm sorry about Nikki," he said, wiping her tears with his
handkerchief. His own eyes watery. "That little girl made my
life worth living. We had planned to retire in Atlanta just so
we could be near you and her."

"I never knew that," she said quietly.

"That's 'cause we never talk." He seemed unsure now. His
voice dropped self-consciously. "I thought we could change
that. I love you, Mia."

"I love you, too," she said, resting her head on her father's
shoulder.

The simple gesture brought back reminders of Adam. How
good it had felt to be with him. How special he always made
her feel. It had been a month since she left him.

According to Star, he was busier than ever, hardly in town
because of his new business venture with a hotel businessman.

But what hurt most was that Star said he never, ever mentioned her. She blocked the pain, closing her eyes, focusing on
taking her next breath.

Moving back to Chicago was supposed to make her feel
better. So far it hadn't worked. The pain lay too deep.

"Mia?"

"Mmm?"

"I've been in love for thirty-seven years. With your mother,"
he added with a cough, clearing his throat.

"What I'm trying to say is that one bad marriage doesn't
make you exempt from ever loving again." He clapped his

hands together and looked at her. "Do you get what I'm saying?" he asked gruffly.

That old familiar rush curled around her, and she looked up, but Adam wasn't there.

"His name is Adam," she said, closing her eyes, a mental picture of him forming.

Tall, soft-spoken, generous smile, beautiful lips, great hands, and a gigantic heart. *Why did I leave?* she wondered, but bit her tongue when the answer was before her.

"I left him because I was scared."

"Of what?"

"Of making the same mistake twice. I thought Derrick was a good guy, too," she went on. "Of disappointing him. Adam wants children," she finally said, getting to the real problem. "And it terrifies me."

Her father nodded. The school bus pulled up and they watched the children cross the street. Three girls chattered, and as they passed the house they waved.

"Hi, Mr. Jacobs," they said, singsong.

"Hello, ladies," he responded, which caused them to giggle.

"We're girls, silly," one replied, and they kept going down the street.

Mia smiled. "Friends of yours?"

"Yeah." He smiled and pointed to the corner. "I used to have physical therapy in the afternoon for my hip. I would get home just before the school bus and see people running the sign. One day, a car hurtled through, just missing the girls."

He struggled up. "So I started crossing them myself and having a patrol car wait right at that corner. Now all I have to do is sit here. Those kids are not a replacement for Nikki, but I don't miss her as much having them around."

In his own way, her father was telling her to get on with her life.

He fiddled with a half dead Boston fern plant. "There's another reason why I came out here."

Mia stood beside him and plucked rows of dead leaves from the plant. Soon she had a bunch of brown leaves in her hand.

"Derrick is being processed and taken to a prison out of state, tonight. I couldn't work it out any other way. He's holding out information because he wants to see you. Honey, it's only for five minutes."

Taking a moment to absorb what her father had said, Mia brushed the twigs into the plastic garbage can.

"Five minutes," she verified.

"And you won't ever have to see him again."

"Let's go," she said, and walked inside to get her purse.

"I'll meet you at the car in two seconds. I have to get my wallet and hat."

Derrick's appreciative gaze did nothing for her.

Mia cringed and counted to ten before she sat at the glass-partitioned booth and picked up the phone.

Mia couldn't understand why she was there.

"What do you want, Derrick?"

"It's been a long time, Mia. No hello?"

"You had four years of my life to make small talk. Now you have five minutes. Don't waste your time. What do you want?"

She could hardly focus on his face, the typewritten confession he gave to police still pounding through her mind. He had been drunk, just as she always suspected.

The typewritten pages were factual and impersonal, and stung like a sharp slap.

Nikki had fallen into the pool and drowned because of his negligence. He'd pled guilty to involuntary manslaughter, but was serving the sentence concurrently with his other charges.

Mia glanced obviously at her watch and rose to leave.

"Okay, okay," he said, folding his hands in front of him. "I wanted you to come here so that I could see you. I didn't want the kid, but I didn't want her to drown, either."

"Your sympathy is touching. But two years too late."

"I was having problems. You were getting to be a big shot doctor," he whispered with feigned awe, then dripped sarcasm. "A regular Superwoman. But my career was sliding in the toilet."

"So you killed our child."

"No," he shook his head. "It just happened. I didn't know she would really try to get in. I was so sleepy from the booze that I must have drifted off. When I came to, I heard you calling me, so I took off and didn't come back until later that night."

She had lived the remaining horror and survived.

"Why did you give yourself up?" she asked, staring at the stranger. His lip curled in what she was sure he thought was a smile. It really was a cross between a grimace and a sneer. "Because it didn't hurt me one way or another to tell. They want the information I have on this stockbroker," he whispered, like they were sharing a secret. "The information he's given out to people will blow the roof off local government and private industry. And I have what they want."

He smoothed his hand over his neat haircut. On the outside he looked like Mr. Honest Citizen. On the inside was a sick, disease-infested individual. Much to her horror, he went on.

"I thought that once I beat this, we could be together again. Just you and me. Like the old days. I mean, you might have to carry the load for a while, but I'll be back on my feet soon . . ."

Mia fought the sickening feeling in the pit of her stomach. "I would never, ever get back with you. Not even if you were the last speck of male carcass that occupied space on this earth. You're going straight to hell, where you belong."

Mia stood up and walked away without a backward glance. She didn't breathe until the warm sunshine bathed her face. Her father held her hand.

It had all come together back there. Seeing Derrick had been all the closure she needed. There was a man out there who loved her, someone who had seen her at her worst and her best and loved who she truly was. She loved him, too, she realized, and walked faster.

"Dad, I need to make a stop. Then I need a ride to the airport."

"I'm way ahead of you. I called the airport while you were talking to him." He motioned to the prison with his head. They climbed in the car. "You don't have time to stop if you're going to catch a flight that leaves in sixty-two minutes. What do you want to do?"

She glanced out the back window as the prison got smaller and smaller. Mia turned around. She had spent too much time looking back.

"I can quit my job just as easy from Atlanta as in person. The result will be the same. I want that flight."

He smiled. "That's my girl."

The fragrant scent of the house surrounded her as she walked in through the front door. Mia turned and waved to J.R. and Star, who had picked her up at the airport. It was good to see them so happy, especially since they had just gotten news that Star was pregnant.

Mia closed the door and grew more nervous as her heels clicked on the wooden floor. She slipped off her shoes, her feet welcoming the plush pile carpet.

The house was noisy in its emptiness and she searched each room, lingering in Adam's. He wasn't inside the house.

The gardens. Mia hurried down the stairs and through the sunroom to go outside, but was disappointed when she couldn't find him.

She passed the pond and was surprised to see all the fish gone. In the place was fresh soil.

Disappointed, she went back into the house and settled on the black leather couch where they had their first entanglement. It was funny now, as the smooth material embraced her. They had been far more intimate, and would be in the future, if she had her way, she thought drowsily.

Mia stretched, coming awake slowly. It took a moment for her to get her bearings, and she sat up, smoothing her hand over her face. The realization that she wasn't alone hit her after a few moments. She guessed it rather than saw him. He sat in a chair off the side of the couch where she'd lain, but it was the charged air that alerted her to his presence.

"Adam?" she said, and turned, and he was there.

Longing crept through her veins when she snapped on the table lamp. He looked better than ever, and she slowly got off the couch and walked to him.

Her eyes remained fixed as she sank on the ottoman in front of his feet.

"Hi," she said.

He didn't respond.

"I came back because I want to give us a chance."

Mia moistened her lips and hurried on. "The reasons I left were rather complicated, but they don't matter anymore." She folded her hands in her lap. "Derrick, my ex-husband, confessed to involuntary manslaughter in Nikki's death."

Her voice dipped. "I lost it. It was like losing her all over again, and it hurt so bad." He still hadn't said anything, but a glimmer of light shone in his eyes.

"Anyway, running home wasn't the answer, either. I missed you. I missed this house. I missed my friends." She placed her hands on his knees, leaning toward him.

"I love you, Adam. Plea—" her voice broke. "Please forgive me and say you'll love me forever."

A single tear trickled down her face, and he reached up and plucked it off her chin. Taking her hand in his he led her outside, around to the side of the house that had once been woods.

A large piece had been flattened, and an oddly shaped wooden structure sat in the center.

"What is this?" she asked, facing him. His hands slid up the back of her arms, warming her.

"First tell me you love me."

Her heart rejoiced at the first words he'd spoken to her in a month.

"I love you, Adam," she declared softly.

"I don't think those trees over there could hear you."

"I love you!" she shouted, laughing. He hugged her to him.

He grew serious. "Now tell me you'll marry me."

"I'll marry you and make you the happiest man on earth."

She laced her fingers behind his neck.

His lips tasted so sweet, and Mia wasted no time reacquainting herself with them. When they broke away moments later, she was breathless with desire and so was he.

"Will you tell me what that is, now?"

"It's for our children. It's for us." He stripped the bow from her hair and plowed his fingers through it, claiming her lips again.

He whispered raggedly against her ear. "I knew you would be back. That's why I built it. Because I never gave up on you. We're together now and forever."

Tears glistened in her eyes, and she went into his waiting arms.

The brisk wind blew as the couple kneeled down, tending to the graves of their beloved. They smiled lovingly at each other, gathering the blown leaves and twigs. Adam and Mia stood and clasped hands, her head coming to rest on his broad shoulder.

Mia embraced her husband of one day and tugged on his hand, urging him to come. They had a plane to catch.

"Adam, I have a surprise for you," she said, her voice hushed.

"What's the rush, baby? We still have two hours before our plane leaves for the Islands." Mia smiled tenderly. "I want to show you something."

Hurrying ahead of him, she slid into the driver's seat of the Gold Lexus, and placed the present on the passenger seat.

Adam curled his tall frame into the car and sat on something lumpy. "What's this?" he asked, pulling it from under himself. He stared at the size 0 infant shoes.

"Who? Us?"

She smiled, shaking her head. "Not yet."

Mia rubbed his leg suggestively. "Remember when you said we would wait until I was ready to start trying? Well, I'm ready."

She could hear the emotion in his voice as he crushed her to him. "Mia Jacobs Webster, I love you. You're the best thing that ever happened to me."

She smacked kisses all over his face, settling tenderly on his lips. "I love you, baby. Forever."

Dear Reader:

My dream has come true!

I've always dreamed of being an entertainer. Moving crowds of people with my voice or actions played in my mind from the time I was a small child. I can't sing nor act, but I've learned I am a storyteller. Amazed best describes how I feel. Blessed bespeaks what I am.

At thirty-two, married, with three children, I never imagined I would be starting a new career, so it's been a delightful surprise.

Writing has afforded me the opportunity to give light to my ideas, voice to people unseen by others, and life to a goal. I appreciate everyone who has read *Now or Never. Look* for my second release in September of 1997.

Correspondence is welcome. Please enclose a SASE. My address is PO Box 956455 Duluth, GA 30136-9508.

About the Author

My name is Carmen Green and I am a native of Buffalo, New York. I graduated from Bennett High School, then went on to complete a bachelor of arts degree in English from Fredonia State University College in Fredonia, New York.

I lived in Rochester, New York, and Syracuse, New York, before relocating to Atlanta, Georgia in 1988. However, that move was only temporary.

I left Georgia with my husband and moved to Chicago, where I lived for four years. Moving back to Atlanta in 1992 was a dream come true. It allowed me the opportunity to stay at home and raise my three children.

I began writing in 1994, and soon after sold my first novel, *Now or Never*. My second story, *Whisper To Me*, a novella, will be released in the *Silver Bells Anthology* for Arabesque in December 1996.

My third novel, tentatively titled *Silken Love*, will be released in September 1997.

My interests include traveling, reading, aerobics, and writing.

Look for these upcoming Arabesque titles:

December 1996

EMERALD FIRE by Eboni Snoe
NIGHTFALL by Louré Jackson
SILVER BELLS, an Arabesque Holiday Collection

January 1997

ALL THE LOVE by Bette Ford
SENSATION by Shelby Lewis
ONLY YOU by Angela Winters

February 1997

INCOGNITO by Francis Ray
WHITE LIGHTNING by Candice Poarch
LOVE LETTERS, Valentine collection

TIMELESS LOVE

Look for these historical romances in the Arabesque line:

BLACK PEARL by Francine Craft (0236-0, $4.99)

CLARA'S PROMISE by Shirley Hailstock (0147-X, $4.99)

MIDNIGHT MOON by Mildred Riley (0200-X; $4.99)

SUNSHINE AND SHADOWS by Roberta Gayle (0136-4, $4.99)